The
Cat Did It

Claude Beccai

Published by:

FriesenPress
Suite 300 – 852 Fort Street
Victoria, BC, Canada V8W 1H8

www.friesenpress.com

Distributed to the trade by The Ingram Book Company

Table of Contents

For my beloved sister Jacqueline, my childhood patient listener and staunch supporter, and Manuelle, Kevin and Dominique, my children and stern teachers.

Acknowledgments

My heartfelt thanks to all those around me who never failed to encourage me in my endeavour to finish this book tirelessly prodding and demanding that I shake off my aloofness to complete it so they could find out what happens. First and foremost my sister Jacqueline with her innate wisdom and infinite patience. My daughters Manuelle and Dominique who proofread the document and commented intelligently, correcting my Gallicisms with a smile. Sonya Rodier as a first serious reader whose enthusiasm for my prose gave me more confidence to have it publish, Glen Sherk and his sensible comments. Gerry Knapp who generously edited without a complaint for my lousy punctuation habits, he even went through the expense of a red pencil to do so. My dear friend Geneviève Leidelinger, quite contrary, who inspires me to see the world from a different perspective. The regretted Mathilda, the cat featured on the front cover, and Diane Skinner Rajotte the photographer extraordinaire who took the picture. Willy Litzenberg who claims he enjoyed the story but hates the title. The two little girls, Kali and Naomi, my granddaughters, whose fresh outlook on life inspired me.

The I and the Me

I am bored. Bored, bored... Nothing really happens to me anymore. I would welcome some excitement. I am not talking about the day to day weather report, or listening to the neighbour being caught in traffic on the highway or even two years ago the other neighbour having her purse snatched in a supermarket; it's a bit stale yet she still talks about it. No, I wish something would happen to me personally like winning the only ticket worldwide to fly into space, or discovering that I have the uncanny ability to whisper to frogs or even that a big TV personality, like the one with the protruding chin and the beady eyes, has fallen head over heels in love with me. Whatever. It does not matter. But I need to get my blood pumping faster for a while even if it is not recommended for longevity. Maybe I should rob a bank; the planning of it would keep me busy and amused until I am totally decrepit and its execution would possibly take me to jail which is not a bad alternative to the otherwise politically correct and fearsome palliative care ward.

'*Bored*' is dangerous as any social worker or psychologist will tell you. It leads to mischief. If you don't want children doing stupid things, keep them occupied. The same principle is true for old people. Organize carpet bowling, wheelchair square dancing, etc.

I read this book the other day about the power of Now by Eckhart Tolle. I could try that. It is going to be difficult because, like many people my age I have a regrettable knack to drift into the past. Nevertheless it might be a cool and challenging project and it does not cost anything. I would take it upon "Me" to live in the Now.

I hope the lofty "I" will forgive the "Me" when I linger surreptitiously in the Now of Then. The "I" is a pretentious entity beyond reach ofttimes. It is supposed to melt in with the universe; it has no name and is generally a cold bastard. The "Me" has a name, "Clara". It feels anger, even rage, envy, discouragement, can be tickled pink by a compliment, lies with or without shame, has a bothersome bunion, cries and laughs idiotically at the wrong moment, has strong opinions about almost everything and might forget these opinions when convenient to the moment. A turn-coat, an anti-hero, a run-of-the-mill nobody who happens to have been liked and even loved, though mildly and lives now in limbo land.

The "Me", Clara, I love and loathe all at once. So, what follows is my "Now". May it enlighten the "Me", should I say the "Mes" for I discovered a few of those, and keep the pestering "I", ever so present, silently in the background!

I am going to acknowledge what is happening "Now", observe my reactions to everyday events with as much honesty as I can muster but of course, I don't think I can help it, continue to live under the heavy shadow cast by my own private lore.

Meet the felon

Tuesday Afternoon, I am starting the Now stuff:

Coming back from a long walk on the sea wall, a block away from the building where I live I see it rolling lustily on the bit of grass in front of the plush building next to the one in which I live. I stop and admire its amazing blue eyes, its lush fur and I walk on. The cat follows me. So I keep talking to it. Once at my door I bid it good day. The cat sits looking at me. I tell it to go home but as soon as I open the front door it slips into the lobby. I have to let the door shut to try to get it out again but each time I try to catch it, it escapes me. This goes on for a good twenty minutes until I give up, call the elevator and decide that eventually the next tenant who goes out will let the cat return to its rightful owner. Once in my apartment I forget about it, turn the TV on to catch some interesting program and promptly fall asleep on the sofa. Upon waking, it is time for the evening news then a late snack and to read the next chapter of my current book in bed before slumbering the night away.

Wednesday Morning:

Mornings the daily newspaper is delivered to my apartment door. I open the door and the damned same cat from yesterday is sitting on it. I have always had decent relationships with cats. When I meet an unknown feline, we appraise each other with an open mind then we usually approve and go our separate ways. I never had the urge to own a cat and I never wanted to be owned by one. This one is definitely a party pooper. It swiftly scurries past my door and runs under my bed.

My apartment is what is called in these parts a one bedroom. It consists of a living room with adjoining kitchen facilities, a bathroom and a bedroom with a few closets. Although very modest it costs me a big chunk of my meager old-age pension. I don't want to move out to cheaper accommodations because I am used to the walls and the neighborhood even though it means that the last days of the month I am on a cat food diet to make ends meet. Thinking of the cat food it's what might have attracted the cat to me in the first place. The smell!

At my age my energy must also be on a tight budget. So after lying on the floor near the bed trying in vain to talk the Cat into leaving, I have to get myself a hot cup of tea and return to my weekly book on quantum physics, fascinating subject by the way. If you want to blow your mind I highly recommend trying to understand this concept and its implications. Then my daily walk to keep my blood flowing. Nothing special to report. I prepare a bowl of synthetic chicken soup; watch Jeopardy, answer some questions a bit ahead of the contestants just to prove to myself that I have not contracted Alzheimer's inadvertently on the seawall. I play a few games of Free Cell on my computer and go to bed. To hell with the cat!

Thursday Early:

At two in the morning I wake up with a weight on my stomach. It's not the chicken noodle soup, but 'It', the Cat. I push it to the side and decide to deal with the problem later on. I am way past the age of emergencies, ASAPs, IfNots, or other threats to keep me on my toes and stupid. Even the ultimate threat of death does not stir me into action anymore. It is a nice feeling to know that whatever happens, nobody can intimidate me anymore. Even when I go to a computer store to browse, the young sales nerds who look at my wrinkles with condescension and talk down to me from the height of their straight spine and their pasty complexion have very little impact on my demeanor.

When I get up the Cat is at the door waiting, I let "It" out, it's gone, and my problem is solved. Nice, because pets are not allowed in my building. Although it is now illegal to forbid pets, I would still have to tackle the superintendent who answers to the board of directors and is nervous about his job. Everything is back to normal; I can get on with my morning routine. The Cat is on my mind, it's been a long time now since anybody took such an interest in me. With the years one tends to get a bit mushy.

Back from my daily walk, the Cat is at my door, same scenario. Somehow it managed to get through the front door, up three flights of stairs to wait at my door. That Cat is a born delinquent. I respect that kind of spirit in anyone. I have never been a stickler for rules and regulations myself. You have got to use a little creativity to get what you want when you want it. That cat has something important to tell me but my fluency in Cat language is extremely limited and to top it off, Cat is a Persian if I am not mistaken. Do Persian cats express themselves differently than Siamese? It would not make any difference for I do not speak Cat Siamese either.

Next Tuesday:

This has been going on for almost a week. I phoned the SPCA, they told me to bring the cat over and surely the owner would eventually reclaim the cat. Well it is the 24th of the month by now and I don't have the money to spare for a cage to travel with the cat. So they take my phone number in case they get a call that fits the situation providing I am not scared to let a stranger in my home or at least have my phone number.

I had a dream last night; my mother was telling me that the price of butter had gone up. This is an omen of rough waters coming soon. My long dead mother is still on a motherly path. That's good to know for she is seldom wrong. She had no sense of humor but she remains a straight shooter. So upon waking I brace myself, the

Cat is licking its paw by my side, the sun is up and soon after the phone rings. The voice is very polite, a bit strained, and identifies itself as a Persian cat owner; it asks for my address and tells me it would come over by eleven if it is not inconvenient. It is not.

Meet the sneak's owner

She shows up on time. Red, yellow and blue three hundred dollar loafers, razor-sharp creased serge navy slacks, gold-ringed diamond studded fingers, manicured hands, pink polo shirt with an exclusive golf club shirt logo, dyed blond tightly permed and sprayed hair, wrinkled face, about my age. She is effusive and thankful. She calls me "My Dear" presents herself as Cynthia Weatherborne and instructs me to call her Cynthia. She is jolly. She bought the Cat for two thousand dollars from the very best cat breeder of the Valley. That cat is the patient of the well known veterinarian homeopath who recommends raw food and has a specialist veterinarian chiropractor in his team. That cat costs so much that I think she should wear it around her neck at all times to enhance her social status.

She takes a quick glance at my unlabelled jeans, my bare feet and my five dollar T-shirt, but then she glances also at the scattered books all over the floor and decides that she is not going to offer me a housecleaning job, instead she tells me that she belongs to a book club and that last month they discussed "The Necklace" from a French author but she forgot the name. She also went to see "The Importance of Being Earnest" staged by the Ladies Auxiliaries of the General Hospital. It was an excellent show. It featured the cousin of the Premier's wife. She does not know how she could learn all those lines and she looked so young on stage that she was amazed. Last year, the same organization staged "Waiting for Something or Other" and that was an awfully boring play with only two male actors, a tall young man whom she later learned is the head of the neurosurgeon's team and did a stint at the Mayo Clinic and a little fellow who must be "Chinese or whatever from over there" and is doing research with stem cells (she called it steam cells) and macular degeneration. – After the show they had a silent auction where she bid on an awful lamp that she later gave to the Salvation Army. There was also a lovely buffet where she met a school friend who had married the daughter of her piano teacher who later died in a car accident leaving him to remarry Aurelle, John Askwith's widow left with a sizable chunk of properties. She keeps name dropping for a good forty five minutes. I tune out. As she leaves with the Cat she talks of inviting me for lunch sometime this week to compensate for all my trouble. That suits me fine. A break from cat food; I hope it will be soon.

Wednesday Afternoon:

The next day the Cat is back at my door. Behind It Marge, the Superintendent's wife, in her flowery frock and her blue fake fur slippers - she is very feminine - an ugly accusing frown on her crooked face.

Is this your new cat? I ask quickly with as innocent a face as I can muster. I know she hates cats. I also know it takes her a while to voice her reproach especially when she is in too much of a rush to adjust her dentures since she was affected with the "Bell Chindrop" as she calls it. She means of course Bell's Palsy Syndrome, that sudden paralysis of one side of the face which if not treated immediately leaves the sufferer with a decidedly crooked face. We had a prime minister once who suffered from the same ailment. He was French Canadian and it did not improve his pronunciation one bit.

Cat is sitting licking its paw methodically. We exchange a knowing look. Cat and I, we have a connection. I also ask if she finally found the super mop as advertised on TV and that she so wishes to get. She is still looking for it. Life is full of unfulfilled desires. I ask about her husband's varicose veins, I comment on the weather and then I ask if there was something she wanted to tell me. She turns around, the cat is gone. She inquires about the noise from the tenant upstairs and I tell her that everything is quiet now that his wife is in the hospital with a black eye and a broken jaw. She leaves and I return to my daily crossword puzzle. I reflect on my dream and decide that I have averted the worst. I commend myself for my cunning and wink at my mother who is furtively farting up on the ceiling by the hanging witch I have put up as decoration above the refrigerator.

As I mentioned before my mother had no sense of humor and also for the first sixty five years of her life she did not have an ass. I was convinced for the longest time that I had been immaculately conceived. Of course eventually with age you start questioning those things. Anyhow by the time she reached the age I am in now she lost some control on her sphincters and the slightest rush move would make her break wind. Instead of being mortified, to my great surprise, the fart would send her in a peal of laughter, all this contained merriment she had dutifully hidden for so long was erupting out of her through all the escape routes her poor old body could afford. The more she laughed, the more she farted until she was in total hysterics, tears in her eyes, rosy cheeks and all signs of debilitating arthritis gone for a while. I read somewhere that one can recognize a sage by his or her sense of humour. So my mother must have intermittently attained the heavenly cheerfulness of the blissful by means of flatulence. I hope to die laughing too, farting or not.

Thursday Morning:

The Persian cat owner calls to tell me that she made a reservation at the Casa di Antonio, the newest restaurant in town with a chef straight from Florence, Spain or somewhere around there, that she has wanted to try for sometime but did not dare go alone. She will pick me up with a taxi at a quarter to twelve, could I be kind enough to wait downstairs in the lobby.

I review my wardrobe and find the appropriate attire, some twenty year old outfit that is, as my mother called it, timeless.

All hell breaks loose

Thursday Noon:

The restaurant is owned by an Iranian, and the chef might have passed through Florence but I am sure he is a Punjab without the turban; the sommelier is of Chinese descent. The clientele is just as cosmopolitan. The head waiter lights a candle. Nice crockery, the menus and wine lists are leather bound. Cynthia, more bejeweled than the first time I met her, is a gracious hostess. I won't be bashful choosing from the menu. It's not often I get an expensive meal and I plan to milk it. Whatever its name I am renaming that cat Providence.

I order half a cantaloupe with prosciutto, endives braisées, and I will have the crème brulée for dessert. We share half a bottle of Valpolicella. The service is efficient, Cynthia is voluble telling me about all her acquaintances, I have no idea who they are but I keep nodding as if I am listening, I am too busy enjoying the meal. I confess I am grossly retarded on the subject of Who's Who. Everything comes with a price including freebies. As we are starting on the main course I notice a young man, who does not seem to belong to the staff, passing a second time by our table. But then I look out the window, there is a black SUV moving slowly as if looking for a parking spot. The two men inside nod at the man who passed by our table. Somehow I become aware that something is wrong. I don't like the look of this. It must be the dream. The car window lowers, I grab Cynthia by her sleeve and I force her to duck with me under the table as I hear gun shots, scattered glass, screams. It all happens in a few seconds. Cynthia's mouth is agape with a little sliver of spit joining her slacked lips and a limp asparagus lying on her skirt between her legs. There are some people on the floor bleeding, moaning, two are obviously dead.

Under the table Cynthia is pumping my hand and whispers "Let's get out fast; we have not seen anything". It takes me a moment to compute but eventually I can see her point. If the shooters are bold enough to do what they just did in plain daylight, what would they do to two old biddies that can identify them? So ever so slowly we crawl on all fours to the closest door which happens to be the kitchen. It's empty. The floor is greasy, the door to the freezer is ajar, there must be someone hiding in there. Another brave one trying to cool off perhaps.

Now we are out in the back alley; by the garbage cans that smell like the devil. Cynthia brushes herself, utters a little nervous laugh, refreshes her lipstick that by some unfathomable reason, she had kept in her hand. She has a big hole in her stocking right at the knee. "Well, MyDear, we will have to come another day to claim our dessert" she says with trembling lips. My respect for her is greatly enhanced. You have to give credit to her kind of people; they have an amazing instinct for survival.

I regret that I did not have time to savour my crème brulée and to top it all off, I lost my left shoe. It makes me quite sad. I had bought these shoes fifteen years ago, just two weeks before my husband shot himself dead because of gambling debts. They were lovely black suede pumps with a plastic ruby on top. They make my feet look pretty smart, almost coquettish. Sometimes to remember that I was not always as poor as an alley cat I would even wear them to go down to the laundry room, a shared facility for the residents of the complex.

Cynthia emits a little muffled cry; she forgot her purse at the restaurant. Meanwhile I spot the black hood of a car slowly appearing at the other end of the back alley. Sirens are blaring, the police have arrived. We must get away; soon the newspaper reporters will be here too. I don't know what to fear most, the media, the police or the gangsters who are right now scanning the alley ever so slowly. I don't possess any credit cards and there were three dollars and thirty six cents left on my account the last time I checked. It is the 26th of the month after all, my pension check is not deposited before the 28th this month, three working days before the end of the month and this is August.

I forcefully wedge both of us between the wall and the large garbage cans. We share the space with a cloud of flies hovering over the carcass of a rat, several used condoms, and a haggard fellow in the process of pushing a needle in his arm, there is a "fuck you" sign scribbled shyly on the back of the garbage can, the meek retaliation of a victim. Back alleys can tell a lot of stories. Mostly gruesome. Cynthia is shivering against my back, I beg her not to faint. The SUV slows even more perhaps sensing some activity nearby; the fellow with the needle peaks his head out and collapses without much of a sound. His right eye is gone with what I guess is part of his brain if he had any left. As soon as the car disappears we slip away. Cynthia is very ladylike; she has a stiff upper lip. We enter the back door of a furniture store, thread our way through it and plan to exit through the front door not without her mentioning that she bought some knick knacks from there a couple of months ago. As a matter of fact the owner or what seems to be the owner greets her with open arms. Greedy store keepers love suckers especially the ones with diamond studded necklaces even when escorted by a one foot shod companion. She returns the greeting as if nothing happened. I don't know any more which one I like best the Cat or her. I could do with a friend but she is certainly not the one I would have chosen had I had my pick. When you start believing that you have somewhat mellowed from the youthful insufferable way of judging people you come to the ugly realization that young fools make old fools. The classifying mania most of us share when it comes to who is who is deeply embedded in our psyche. Here is this lovely old goat with a lot of grit, a true sense of style when it comes to clothes and I was ready to write her off as an idiot not worthy of attention. I am the idiot! There, now that I have admitted my guilt; let's get on with it. Cynthia, you trooper, you dear, shall we play on? Oh, I feel all schmaltzy!

We decide of a common accord to go and rest a little on a bench in the park across the street. Just so as to get our bearings. The idea is to return home. Cynthia's cell phone was in the purse she left under the table in the restaurant and I never got around to spending the money to get one. Walking is out of the question with my bare foot which I have wrapped with Cynthia's scarf to look like it's in some kind of a cast. Of course I limp. We must use the public transit system dodging the security since she can't afford to pay for the fare and I can't help her there.

Cynthia has never used the subway; so it's time to give her a crash course on the dos and don'ts in public transit. Take off all your jewelry, wear flat heeled comfortable shoes and cheap sporty clothing. Important ID or credit cards in a safe pocket out of view, don't look anybody in the eyes, don't look scared, don't count on anybody helping you if you are being attacked, beware of hooded youths. Avoid the rush hour crowd. If you follow these simple rules the subway is pretty safe and can actually be enjoyable.

I have a senior monthly pass which is very cheap to get at the beginning of the month. It is also very convenient. I use the subway all the time just for refreshing larks. In our city the subway runs above ground most of the time. When it's raining or too cold to walk I like the scenery and rubbing elbows with people. Sometimes I even strike up a conversation with a passenger. Most users are very nice people but the odd one can be dangerous to women particularly old ones.

We trade jackets to confuse anyone who might identify us. I mess up my hair, and tell her that I will act senile or demented with my one shoe and she should act as if she is escorting me; people try to avoid crazies. She puts her rings, bracelets, and necklace in her bra. We now look like two cronies escaped from a hospice for the light-headed elderly. I give her my transit pass. There are two police cars at the station but they hardly notice us. Cynthia is positively thrilled. I think we are starting to form a workable team that could be the beginning of a lot of fun. Now that the shock of what happened has somewhat subsided, she can't believe her luck to be living such an adventure and I concur. We must have been utterly bored with our lives.

Strange how callous one can be when in the midst of action and scared. We have just witnessed an incredible act of violence and all we think about is to save our butts. Let it be known that it never crossed our minds to humanely reflect on the poor victims. All we could think of was to run, run, run limping or not.

Smart moves

On the train we had agreed to go to my place first, it was safer since the forgotten purse would by now be in the hands of whoever found it first, the gangsters or the police. Most likely the gangsters. It would be a bit safer in the hands of the police but we would be asked to be witnesses, a dangerous thing to do against such bold criminals. We enter through the garage door at the back of my building. Cynthia wants a change of clothes she admits bashfully that she has wet herself. As I rummage through my stuff to outfit her with some clean garb, we try to organize a plan of action. The idea is to disappear for a while until the police find the hoodlums. We don't want to be witnesses to anything. If these guys feel safe enough to open fire at noon in a busy restaurant downtown who knows what they are capable of doing to those who can identify them? We need money, I will go alone to Cynthia's place, she has a spare key at a neighbour's. She phones him to make sure that he is home and informs him that she has hired a new cleaning lady who is supposed to arrive shortly yet she forgot to leave a key with her, she is retained at her friend's for a while longer and would he be kind enough to let me in. She calls me Wilma. I put my runners on, my jeans and a kerchief to cover my hair. I get a pail and a broom to look the part and I leave her in the shower stall. The pail will be handy to bring back whatever I find useful and the broom can serve as a weapon. I should have planted a nail in the handle for good measure.

The neighbour's name is Malcolm but he instructs me to call him Macky, he is a flourish older guy, with salon curled hair, he wears pink spandex pants that match his lipstick and when he turns around to get the key you can't help but notice the alluring swing of his lower back. Macky is a gem. I can be a warm-hearted mellow hag when I put my mind to it. I can't let go of my wits when it's all I've got left.

As I cautiously enter Cynthia's condominium apartment all is quiet. Lovely old furniture, lots of doodads, beautiful large windows tastefully clad in draperies. I start looking for some clothes in the walk-in closet off the bedroom but then I decide to look for money first. She told me that she keeps some in a rice jar in the kitchen to pay the housecleaner cash and for other emergencies. I retrieve a sizeable wad and head back to the bedroom where I have left the pail and the broom when I hear a click at the entrance door. I slide into the closet just in case. Maybe it's Macky; I can hear more than one set of feet shuffling on the carpet. I bury deep in the wardrobe and cover myself with a fur coat. Someone is getting nearer. I pee in my pants. A noise, a long loud "Fuuuuckkkk", a lamp or something breakable crashes, and the muffled sound of a gunshot. Whoever is in the room just shot the broom? A very vindictive guy that I hope won't find me. I am hot, I am wet and I am shaking all over with the picture of the back alley junky's disfigured face in my mind. I am far from the cool cucumber I so desperately try to be, and no I don't want to die.

A shout from the other room it seems, "Come on I got it!" it says. Good or bad? The fellow nearest me leaves the room. Good. Then a door slams shut. Better. I disentangle from the fur coat, and grab haphazardly some clothes wrap them in the coat; I carry the bundle as if it were a huge pet cat. The money is in my wet panties. I hear the elevator stop; I wait a moment and leave down the staircase as

I have seen it done in lots of police shows on TV. You never know when these shows will equip you with useful tips. Fifteen flights of stairs is a lot of steps. In my frazzled state of mind it leaves me breathless. My heart is ticking so loud I am afraid it will burst. I decide to go all the way to the basement garage. Wrong move. I see a car that looks uncannily like the one in the alley spin its way out. I bravely keep hidden behind a BMW. Of course they have Cynthia's keys and can come back anytime.

I can't wait to tell Cynthia all about it, how I risked my life and on and on but on my way home I stop by a convenient bench on the sidewalk, my turban is askew and I don't care. I must have fallen asleep for when I open my eyes the sun has gone down. It must be late. The cat is looking at me. This time I feel like giving him a good kick in the ass. I will rename It, Catastrophe, Kata for short.

I have to rush home, Cynthia must be beside herself. The cat is at my heels but I am not talking to him. He is nothing but bad news. As I get in, Cynthia is humming contently "Oh my darling Clementine" wrapped in my old bathrobe. She spots the cat, kneels down and exclaims: "Oh my darling Winston, you found me. What a precious little thing you are! Coochee, coochee coo!" or something of the sort. I am dumbfounded. I just single-handedly rescued her from vicious, mean baddies and all she thinks about is to sing Clementine and tickle the cat whose name I don't like.

I don't like her choice of names, "MyDear", "Wilma", and now "Winston" I am not going to tell her anything, I am going to pout in the bathroom and that's it. Besides I need a shower because I stink maybe worse than I did after I found Edgar, my husband with an ugly hole in his right temple and all his debts for me to honour. I peed in my pants then too. Not that I did not like Edgar, he was a charming fellow but you could not trust him when it came to money. I even had to pay for my own wedding ring and his burial. Edgar was a bum, she is a nitwit and I am a patented fool to have entertained the thought that she could be my friend. I don't want friends, I don't need friends, I am a mean old bitch and I like it that way. I am not going to be a dope anymore. Look where it got me losing my business to creditors for loving a guy who deserted me in the worst way! I am so mad I think I am going to throw the damned cat out the window. Now lost in my anger I climb into an ice cold shower. I had forgotten to turn on the hot water. All a-shiver I adjust the taps so nice hot water trickles down my back washing my frustration away.

"I prepared some lovely sardine sandwiches, 'MyDear'" pipes Cynthia through the door. I am hungry but I wonder where she found the sardines along with the bread. She borrowed them from the superintendant she says, Marge the cat hater! I still have a lot to learn.

"What a lovely lady she is this Marge, I told her all about Winston and she was most enthusiastic. I found cheap cat food in your cupboard so I used some, I hope you don't mind. You never told me you had a cat too."

Next move

I must admit Cynthia has a lot of spunk. She is eating the sardine sandwich with knife and fork, sipping a little tea now and then from my best cup while listening to my account. I don't fail to embellish it to my advantage stressing my cunning and presence of mind. I won't tell her about the nap on the bench or the peeing in my pants. I explain that I washed the money because I had kept it in my underwear. I don't stray far from the truth though. When I inquire about her relationship with Macky she calls him a dear-dear treasure of a fellow, they have the same hairdresser; a lot of the knick knacks she buys on his advice. He used to be a real estate agent and made a pile of money; he decided to retire last year. His partner left him for a younger man and he is desolate, such a shame! Thinking of him she is sure he could help. She jumps off the sofa with the agility of a teenager, grabs the phone and dials his phone number before I can voice any objections.

"Please don't say anything over the phone!"

She shushes me, winks and "Hello, my beloved Macky I am having tea with a dear friend of mine who lives right around the corner. I am sure you would love to meet her. Won't you come join us if you are not doing anything special? On the way would you be kind enough to grab some of those lovely blueberry tarts at Thomas Haas? Bring eight or ten of them. He opens late today. Bring a tin of sardines and a loaf of bread too, please. I will explain later. Come as you are, this is an impromptu party. Good, see you soon! Toodleloo!"

Then she gives him directions for my place. I am petrified. I have not had a visitor for the past three years and now I will have a crowd of unknowns invading my privacy. All that because of the blasted cat that is sprawled on my feet purring contentedly. I want my peace; I want to go back to my books, my computer, my favorite TV show, my bed.

It is also true that something has to be done. We need a plan of action. What did the hoodlum mean when he said "I've got it" and left with his broom-shooter pal. Did he find my address? When are they going to show up? We are not safe here. Macky seems like a nice enough fellow but I doubt he has any competence for what is required here.

Half an hour later Macky shows up with two shopping bags Cynthia jumps delighted and gives him two pecks on his shriveled cheeks. Macky is a nice looking man almost as nice looking as Edgar but softer, more polished. He is wearing a fashionable beige summer suit, an open-collared shirt and white leather loafers; he extends his hand towards me and tentatively says "Wilma?"

"Oh no dear this is Clara. Wilma was to hoodwink the enemy." She emits a little fart of merriment.

"We have a lot to tell you!" Cynthia cuts in and sits him in my favorite spot.

All a-flutter she serves each of us a tart playing hostess while telling it all, about the cat, me, the restaurant, the escape on all fours, the junkie's fate, the train trip and my adventure or rather misadventure at her place while Macky makes appropriate oohs and aahs, rolls his eyes, crosses his legs left over right and right over left all the while elegantly balancing his plate of blueberry tart in one hand, the spoon stuck in the corner of his mouth. I am totally left out of the conversation. I am peeved. It is true though that she does a much better job than I would with my pernicious habit of always wanting to come up on top. To appear as a tough cookie when most of the time I end up as a victim. I twist stories to make believe I am in control. Sometimes I try to stop but by then I am so entangled in my boastful yarns and I enjoy it so much that it's impossible. Luckily for me I have never come to believe what I tell. Cynthia is a better player than I am, I should hate her for this but this time even though I pout, I listen. There is still a lot of learning for me to do. Never too late.

After all the expected exclamations such as "That's extraordinary!", "What is the world coming to?" "Our city that was so peaceful!" Macky turns serious and matter of fact. I did not think he had it in him but after all if he had a career in real estate he must have been on the ball sometime.

Has Cynthia taken care of her credit and bank cards? That's almost the first thing she did after her shower. She must pass by the bank tomorrow morning to pick up new ones. Impressive for somebody I took for a ditzy aging blonde. She does not have any ID with her so Macky is going to call a friend of his to accompany him to Cynthia's apartment to get the necessary papers and bring them back here very early tomorrow morning. Cynthia instructs him on where to find the stuff. We count the money I brought back from my expedition. We have three hundred and sixty dollars. Not bad. A whole month of food for me and some.

Macky is now pacing the floor in my living room. Strange, his lower back is not swinging this time. All the same he stops in front of the mirror to rearrange a curl in his blondish dyed mane and turns around suddenly.

"You two can't stay here overnight; as a matter of fact we should leave immediately. You will come to my place until we figure out what to do next."

Cynthia is not convinced, she says that she promised to return the tin of sardines and the bread to dear Marge tonight and also that since the 'baddies' know where she lives they might be waiting for her to return to her place, they might even be in the lobby now since they have the keys.

Macky very theatrically hits his forehead with the palm of his hand.

"I've got it! We should all take an Alaska cruise! How about that you guys? Ten days secured, eating like pigs and watching whales go by while they are not extinct. I am brilliant! Nobody will find us. I always wanted to do that and never got around to it. We will have a super good time in the nicest of company if I can say so myself. It won't cost an arm and a leg. I know a chap who is in the travel business and can get us last minute deals. "

He is beaming. Cynthia, smiling gives little claps of applause and jumps to kiss Macky. I am the party pooper. Whatever the deal, it's out of the question on my budget. I frown fearing abandonment on their part. These two are financially sound, I am not. I can see that once again I will be left alone to fend for myself. All this because of the Cat, I should have handed it to Marge's husband to make a stew and shoe laces out of its intestines. Ron is his name, that Marge's husband, and he is a pretty rough guy. He used to be a logger in the back country, Marge was the camp cook. Sometimes the food was not delivered and the guys had to make do with what was around. Ron learned a few tricks while back there until a trunk fell on his leg. He had to retire with a gimpy leg. That's how he became a reluctant superintendant.

I am not a totally inept nerd. If there is something I know how to do it is to listen when people tell me their stories. As it is, it must be written on my face because all I have to do is walk out my door and whatever dude is passing by stops and starts talking to me, even the bloody cat saw that. Maybe I should wear a burkah, which would also be very convenient if I happened to have a wart on the nose. I hate the cat, its owner and her jolly friend. I hate the world, I hate myself.

While I was silently pondering my resentment, Macky was on the phone, business like. He delicately replaces the receiver on its support, smacks his lips and starts dancing around the living room with Cynthia in his arms. As they twirl there is a knock at the door. We fall dead silent. I tiptoe to the door and look through the peep hole. I see Marge's grossly deformed face through the lens as if her already skewed mug needed that! I turn around and whisper her name. Cynthia rushes to the door, opens it wide:

"Dear dear Marge you are just the person I wanted to see! Please sit down and have a cup of tea with us. I have got your sardines but first have a taste of these lovely tarts I got them brought up especially for you. There are two more for you and your handsome husband."

I am dumbfounded; this is the first time in fifteen years that this Marge has ever entered my apartment. There is a cautious smile on her face. To my amazement she looks almost pretty now. She sits down, checks her skirt, pulls it over her knees, crosses her legs; and holds the cup, pinkie straight up, then bites into the tart from the corner of her crooked mouth.

Macky is standing, his right elbow resting on his left fist, his index finger gently tapping his cheeks, fluttering his eyes. I plop on the ottoman studying Cynthia for signs of dementia then I get it, she wants something from Marge, the calculating bloody vixen, and it is not sardines. Macky is on to it. My political correctness is revolted. The sooner I get out of the clutches of these two the better.

Cynthia is cooing now, she looks straight into Marge's eyes and says: "The minute I saw you I knew you were a kind lady that could be trusted. I was wondering if by any chance, if the occasion arises of course, you could look after my Winston when I am away. You see I have to leave him with somebody who charges me an arm and a leg and is not even looking after him properly the poor dear. I would rather leave him with my good friend Clara but she says she is not allowed pets in her suite. Since you are in charge here the matter is different for you. I'd compensate you, it goes without saying, for all the trouble it would cause. Let's say twenty dollars a day plus food expenses."

Marge's eyes are blinking dollar bills. She is trying to gain some time to think, "I would have to ask Ron. He loves cats but I don't know if we have the time."

"I would go as high as twenty five a day if you could manage. "

"When are you thinking of leaving?"

"Very soon now, maybe even tomorrow. You see a dear friend of mine is sick and I was wondering if I should go see her before it's too late if you know what I mean. I would pay in advance of course. Here are two hundred and fifty dollars for ten days if you agree." And she impatiently extends her hand towards me, rubbing her thumb against her middle finger, I wordlessly pass the 'laundered 'money I had retrieved at her place and she starts counting.

Marge's hand reaches for it. Cynthia withholds it and says:"You'd better go and ask Ron. "

"Oh it's OK I'll look after your cat myself. Ron doesn't need to know about it."

There, another lesson from the conniving little bitch. Marge leaves with the tarts, the sardines, the cat, the bread, and the dough. Just like that.

Macky is laughing "Very well done my dear you are the best. Too bad you were not my partner in business. By the way, I have good news. My friend tells me that we can take advantage of last minute bookings on the Norwegian Ruby sailing tomorrow noon. Half price, a real deal. Nobody can find us until things cool down here. We have a lot to do. Come on girls, let's get busy we are off to see the wonders of the Arctic while sipping Vikings' champagne! "

"I am not going", I cut into their frolics, "half price or not I don't have the money." I wouldn't want to go on a cruise even if I had the financial means, besides I have just lost one of my best shoes and my wardrobe is not up to par. Also I have seen the passengers getting off the ships in the harbour many times, walkers and wheelchairs descending the planks. Most of these cruises are packed with octogenarians on their last outing before the big trip and the members of the crew look like relief caregivers to me. I don't like to be jolly and I don't want to learn square dancing. Yet it is not healthy for me to stay here.

The two clowns are all over me now. They offer to lend me the money, to pay half of it themselves, to be repaid by easy installments. They don't want to leave me behind, maybe they don't trust me. I am adamant. Now they are pacing my living room with all their enthusiasm deflated. I go to the bathroom, close the door and sit on the toilet because this is where I get the most inspired and I know they are too well-behaved to follow me.

Toilet seats are great. I don't know why they are not more celebrated; it is assumed that poets and deep thinkers get their ideas while strolling along flowery paths, or lounging under trees and being hit by falling apples but I know better, as you dump a big load off your gut it seems that your mind too gets lighter. It evacuates the junk that was busily clogging your neurons. Have you ever looked at a baby's angelic smile after it soiled its diaper? I believe that if we shipped Ex-lax to the rulers of countries at war we would have a happier world. Constipation is a plague that prevents us from soaring to higher dimensions. All this to say that when I am in a snit I take refuge in the bathroom to liberate myself of unhealthy crap.

I close my eyes in relief; slowly an image emerges from the recesses of my brain. Edgar is beaming, he takes me in a twirl around the room singing, tee lee tee tee lee tee tee and we fall entwined on the sofa. "Oh my darling, we won the jackpot!", he puffs and I see dollar bills flying all around, the mortgage paid, new tires for the car, a state of the art refrigerator that does not wheeze, I sell my little artistic candle business and what the hell we retire to Bali or even to a Greek island with Zorba. I won't forget the two pound plum pudding for my nice neighbour from Wales.

"No, no, my love, it's not money, it's better than money. It's the free and unlimited use of a cottage in the country! Can you imagine us relaxing in the lovely countryside, far from all the buzz?"

No, but I humour him. Anyway it's far from his gambling buddies. A week later, I prepare a picnic and away we go. The cottage is one hundred kilometres east of Prince Rupert on an old logging road. It's a long two-day drive fifteen hundred kilometres away. We could have gone via the ferry from Port Hardy, twenty hours sailing time through the inner passage, a two or three day travel time one way. We spent one night on a bed bug infested mattress in a squalid motel in Prince George with half a dozen greasy donuts, not exactly my idea of a romantic escapade but I am with Edgar and that's what counts. I am a born sucker. We are off to see the "Estate". The cottage is a shack; nobody has been in it for ages it seems. It is one room with an unstable ladder leading to the loft with four spidery cots and some big nails on the walls conveniently placed to hang your niceties I suppose, an outhouse, no running water, a rusty generator that gives off fumes and makes a huge racket when started. There is a large chimney and above it a rifle. There are ants scurrying around the floor and definitely mouse droppings. Edgar is ecstatic. We stayed two days there and drove the long way back with Edgar making plans to refurbish and start a business growing tomatoes on the roof. Eventually he made a deal with a poultry farm to buy their chicken shit for fertilizer. I never went back but if I had a car that's where I would definitely go right now. Nobody could find me. Enjoy the peace and quiet like Edgar used to say.

I leave the bathroom in a much better mood. I have an alternative to the cruise trip to Alaska. After all Prince Rupert is a stone's throw away from Alaska. So I explain and explain. They are polite but very jittery, their mind is made up. Then Macky the negotiator lights up.

"Would you feel upset if you went all by yourself to this cabin?"

"But I don't have a car."

"I could lend you mine, I am sure you are a good driver. I have two cell phones I would let you have one so we could keep in touch at all times."

Meet Tony Whomever

Friday:

That's why I am now driving all by myself, in a very comfortable SUV after seeing them off at the harbour. I am so happy. The road is beautiful, not much traffic, it's sunny almost warm. I am in no rush and I am singing old tunes along with the crooner on the radio. From Prince George on large billboards start appearing on the side of the road warning girls and women of the dangers of hitchhiking. Thirty two girls have disappeared on this road, mostly aboriginal girls, a few as young as fifteen. These girls, probably enticed by the lure of the big cities and the opportunities as exposed on TV, leave their community on specs. None of the crimes have yet been eluci- dated. There are one or more sickos in these parts, serial killers. It is hard to believe in such an amazingly enchanting country side. I do not feel threatened though because I am way past the age of being a target to this kind of violence but I feel for those girls because fifty years ago I could have been one of them.

I sleep in the back of the car to save money but also because I do not want to meet people, I stop once in a while to stretch my legs, gas up, restock on drinking water or some food. One hundred miles from the cabin, in Terrace, I buy what I think I will need to get by for a week: eggs, hot dogs, apples, cheese, coffee and a newspaper. On the front page there is a gruesome picture of the restaurant where the slaughter happened along with some lengthy articles speculating on who could be the authors of such a massacre. The police are searching for two possible witnesses who might be members of the gang, but so far they have had no luck. Strangely enough that does not upset me. I chuckle and imagine putting on my CV: I have been once a suspect in a brutal murder. I try to imagine the face of the fully serious and business like human resources lady upon reading it. Middle management has strictly no sense of humour. At least the ones I have met. They would probably be very polite and say: "Don't call us, we will call you."

Cynthia calls, she is thrilled too. The cabin is luxurious. The crew is very kind and the food is superb. I am glad she is happy with her own crowd of people. I rename the cat Providence, Provi for short and to confuse the enemy.

Upon arriving at the cabin, I park the car well hidden behind some bushes by the road as Edgar had instructed me to do to avoid unpleasant surprises perpetuated by possible drifters looking for loose change or whatnot. I unload my cargo, climb the muddy path to the lodging and find the keys in a tree log. I need some water for tea; so I take a pail and go down to the lake. The water is nice, I take a refreshing plunge. It is getting late; it would be too much trouble to light a fire. Better forget about the tea, anyway I am bushed. A sound night's sleep will do me a world of good. A last trip to the outhouse with the rifle again as instructed by Edgar:" this is bear country don't forget." Not that I would know what to do with the rifle; I have never used one. So the bear is safe. As for me I count on my luck. The outhouse is a rickety contraption full of see-through holes beside the big one in the middle. I sit on a plank and plug my nose. I don't know why but when I plug my nose I also close my eyes. I hear some shuffling; it must be the wind in the trees.

Relax Clara! All the same as I come out I point my gun like I have seen it done on TV by the good guys. I advance stealthily in my night gown and my flip flops scanning for bears. There is a man sitting on the porch reading the paper. I must have sat longer than I thought in the outhouse. No wonder, when you sit in a car as long as I have you kind of get bunged up. The man drops the news-paper raises his hands above his head and says:"Be careful, Little Lady, those things tend to have a mind of their own. If I were you I would lower the gun and talk; if you are too scared to talk here are your car keys, you can always run I will not catch you." And he throws the keys that land at my feet.

I don't feel like running in my underwear, so I lower the gun thinking I could always give him a good whack with the butt if worse comes to worse as it usually does. I'll act as if I am slightly daft. Most men are denser than women but they like to feel supe-rior. It suits us to let them believe it.

"Good, now it's time to tell me your name" he says in a patron-izing voice.

"No, you tell me first. You are the one invading my property", I retort in as affirmative a tone as I can muster. I feel very vulnerable in my flimsy night gown, the one that Edgar liked the most. It is a black lacy thing that must look completely ridiculous on my old body and the flip flops are the ones I bought in Mexico the one time we had invested in a true vacation far from a gambling joint. They are plastic things adorned with a powder blue flower sitting on top of the big toe. You cannot run very fast with those things.

"Invading your property, you have a lot of gumptions, little lady, this cabin is rightfully mine and has been for the past thirty years. What makes you say so?"

As he speaks I notice he has a tic, his left eyelid is blinking, at first I thought he was giving me the eye because of my sexy nightgown. Fortunately I am way past the age of vanity but one has the right to fantasize once in a while. He is a plump fellow at least twenty years younger than me. That would put him in his fifties. He has a round face and a much rounder gut. Take off fifty pounds and he might be handsome. Yet you have to give it to him, he certainly knows how to dress; I swear that's an Armani suit he is wearing, the shoes and the watch match the suit. His tone of voice is confident, not in the least bit aggressive so I relax somewhat.

"My husband, Edgar Vittorio, won the right to take advantage of this cabin whenever he liked. Since he died leaving me all his debts to honour I thought I might as well keep the few privileges he enjoyed. It's only right!"

I pause, he closes his eyes as if he is thinking about what to answer; he shifts position, opens one eye. I think I got him there.

"So you are Edgar's wife, yes I remember now something of the sort. Tell me how did he get the use of my cabin and have you been here with him often?"

"On a gambling bet, and no I just came once with him after he won but he was here very often. I think he took me there so that I would not worry when he was gone. He told me that he worked hard to improve the place"

"Ah, yes at black jack."

"No I am sure it was at Texas Hold'em that's what he always played."

"Of course! You mentioned that he died, how did this happen? I hardly knew him."

"With a bullet in his brain, that's how." I say defiantly.

"Have they found who did it?"

"It was ruled as a suicide. He shot himself in our car, parked in the garage."

"And you, what do you think?"

"Edgar was a fun guy, but a hair brain with a knack to run into mischief; there was a dark side to him that I never understood. Yet I did not think he was that desperate. The day before he died we had celebrated our anniversary, he was all aglow and in the best of moods. He was making plans for us to retire to the countryside. He said he had found a way to put us on the map financially. There was a police investigation and they did not find any clues other than suicide."

I am dumbfounded that I have revealed all this information to a stranger, it must be the environment, I feel Edgar's presence all over and as usual I don't understand what he wants to tell me. I must admit I still resent him almost as much as I loved him this sweetheart of mine.

The sun is down and I am starting to shiver in my flimsy outfit. I wish we would come to an agreement about who is going to stay in the cabin. All this recollection of poor Edgar is not doing me any good.

He stays not moving for a minute or two, gets up and comes towards me with his right hand extended.

"I am Tony, I am sorry about Edgar; please accept my very late condolences. You can stay for the night if you wish, but tomorrow I am expecting company. I will gladly pay for your stay at a motel for a few nights if you wish to explore the region a bit. I would invite you but I am sure you would not enjoy the party if you know what I mean. I do these kinds of parties once in a long while to entertain my clients." and he winks. I don't know what kind of clients he has in mind to entertain in this shabby cottage with his Armani suit but it's none of my business. It takes all sorts. I would indeed be very happy to stay in a comfortable motel for a few nights. Here I cannot even get a decent cell phone connection to reach Cynthia should I need to.

"I wanted to stay a good week over here. It's for my nerves, the doctor recommended peace and quiet." I say cunningly to see if he would fork the expenses that far.

"One week is no problem with me as long as you don't expect to stay at the Ritz. Anyway you won't find anything resembling the Ritz in this area, but a clean place with plumbing, a nice shower, TV and even free coffee in the morning," he says in a suave voice. This guy knows how to talk to women.

Dragging the butt of the rifle on the ground I step forward, shake his hands lightly and announce that if he does not mind I am going to retire and leave in the morning. As a real gentleman he says that I can use the cot upstairs, he will sleep on the sofa and not to worry if I hear some noise, there are a few things he needs to do before hitting the sack. He makes as if to take the gun from me. This is where I draw the line; I tell him I need it in case I want to use the outhouse, just in case there are bears prowling. He does not look happy but he shrugs good-humouredly warning me to be very careful with this thing. He wants to check if it is properly loaded. I tell him I did it when I first arrived. I lied. I would not know how to do it if I had to.

When I finally lie down on the clammy cot under the clammier smelly blanket I am too tired to care, except I take the precaution to keep the shotgun close to me. In a sense I am happy that this strange Tony is around I feel safer. I think I would not have slept as well had I been alone.

Saturday:

I wake sitting straight up. The rotten canvas of the cot splits and folds me in two, my knees against my chest and my feet above my head. In my fall the gun barrel pokes my stomach in a very unpleasant manner. The sun is up so after disentangling myself from the broken cot, I dress hastily and get down the wobbly ladder. Tony is nowhere. On the table a wad of twenty dollar bills, no note. Aside from the money it's as if he had never been here. But I take the hint, gather my things, pick up some of the food I had bought, I think twice about taking the gun with me yet I decide against it, take a big butcher knife instead and head for Macky's car. Once I am a few miles on the road I stop to count my money. Seven hundred bucks! This Tony is a generous fellow, true to his word. Yet I wonder why he would travel with so much cash in his pocket. A guy like that, dressed as he was must have all kinds of credit cards but this is none of my business, I better enjoy the bounty, I mentally thank the Cat, Provi-Kata-Winston who, in a roundabout way, is instrumental in offering me a nice break to my boring routine.

Harvey's Paradise

It has been a long time since I have felt so flush and carefree. The back road is deserted, tall trees keep it shaded, and it's a beautiful day I sing at the top of my voice as off-key as ever. I sing funny songs from my childhood, when I forget the words I make them up. Sometimes it comes out so funny that I break out laughing. Boy, am I in a good mood! That's what money can do to you. No wonder Edgar was always out to get some more, it was to uplift his gloomy spirit. Whenever he had some cash in his pocket, he would dance and smile and blow it in totally useless endeavours. He would buy me clothes I could never wear, take me to restaurants where I could not digest most of the food served, buy hundred dollar bottles of wine that we did not know how to taste. Buy cars that he had to resell a week later for half the price he had paid. I had to hang on to my little candle store to keep food on the table when he was down and out. But he was so much fun. I never regretted being his partner even though I always knew that he was not the faithful guy he claimed to be. He said I was his lighthouse, the one that would show him the way home, and he was my child, my lover, my tears, my rainbow, my life and now that I have buried him I don't feel sad but rather fortunate that he was part of me. That I was able to love with such carelessness makes me feel like a very successful woman.

Never mind if now I am an old decrepit hag only attractive to pure bred cats, I have had bountiful romance to last me till I die.

I am getting nearer populated areas, I just passed a gas station, and a club with a large bill board featuring scantily clad pretty girls dancing nightly. These entertainment spots are always on the outskirts of small towns. Very soon there will be a motel I am sure; I will choose the next one to try to avoid the clientele of the night club. Here it is, a big neon sign with "Vacancy" blinking in red letters. The outdoor swimming pool is empty; grass grows between the broken cement slabs. Not very appealing. Only one truck in the parking lot confirms the vacancy sign. It is called "Harvey's Paradise". Sometimes when it comes to paradise you have got to settle for what is available. Whichever god Harvey is praying to must be a minor one, or he does not pray loud enough. I am not belittling him because I am sure my god might be even less powerful. I take the room for a week, two days to come up here, one day at the cabin and two days to get back I will have been gone almost two weeks, that should be enough to let things cool down and hopefully for the police to find the thugs, at least the ones hunting us down. I pay cash which seems to surprise Harvey. He gives me a discount and I don't ask for a receipt. Normally you can enter the room only after eleven o'clock but seeing as it is not busy today I can enjoy my room right away since I paid cash.

The room is nothing less or more than what I expected. A sagging bed, clean linen though, an older TV, a tiny humming fridge, a hot plate and a table where someone has etched a grinning skull. The walls are decorated here and there with carcasses of squashed bugs. Tsimshians are renowned for their outstanding masks and their most impressive totems poles but they don't seem to have much of a grasp on interior decoration. On top of the TV there are some ads. Leafing through them I find one for Tim Horton's delicious soups and donuts, and one for Lola's luscious affordable massages just two blocks down the road, open 24/7. Lola is a valiant little lady. I assume she is a she.

The TV has only five channels available. I have to get myself some crossword puzzles or something to entertain me, also a newspaper, and take a tour of the town. But I also want to make myself as scarce as possible. You never know what could happen. As I stretch on the bed for my afternoon nap a bit early I sniff the unmistakable whiff of reefer. That's maybe why Harvey told me when he saw me peel the twenties off my wad that should I need anything I could come to him, he has got some good stuff. Edgar used to bring some home and we would enjoy one together after a nice meal. It sure relaxes you better than the pills the doctors give you, it is a bit more expensive but you don't get the side effects of the pills. Why marijuana is illicit I will never know. I read Marc Emery - the king of Pot as he is called, and who is in jail now for having sold cannabis seeds to US citizens - study on the subject and I am pretty convinced that it is a matter of big money and dirty politics. Not for us the poor taxpayers who must pay for the police actions, maintain the prisoners in jail to the tune of $50,000 a year per head, and live in dread of the violence of competing gangs. It keeps criminal lawyers fat mind you. Yet, I have never heard of someone intoxicated on weed beat his wife or his children nor have I ever heard that someone died of an overdose of marijuana. So the law is not geared to protect the population.

During my nap, my mother came to me again, even though she disliked back woods of the country, she told me that it was a cloudy day. The sky is a pure blue, so I dismiss the foreboding and walk out to explore the surroundings, get the paper and treat myself with a famous soup at Tim Horton's where old guys are lacing their coffee with gin from bottles hidden in brown bags and joking with the waitresses. There is nothing in the paper pertaining to the shooting we witnessed.

Prince Rupert people look peaceful enough and cautiously friendly. The region is home to the Tsimshians. Of the 12,000 or so inhabitants, over forty percent are of First Nations origin. That explains Harvey's long jet black hair tied in a pony tail and his high cheek bones. Near the harbour there is a collection of Totem poles that are known artefacts of the Haïda and the Tsimshian. All these recent descendants of aboriginal peoples are still grossly traumatized by the arrival of us, white trash, about 150 years ago. In our usual brutal ways we appropriated their land, killed a lot of them, infested them with small pox eradicating in some cases ninety percent of their village populations. We forbade them to honour their traditions, we made laws to ban potlatches, their way of celebrating their customs, we separated the young children age six to fifteen from their parents by sending them to boarding schools run by religious nuts who abused them both physically and sexually, made them work in their farms and punished them cruelly when they tried to speak their mother tongue. The death rate in these schools was in the range of sixty five percent. When one thinks that in Canada the last residential school as they are called, closed in 1996! All this endorsed by our upright citizens in power, the clergy of various denominations and us the silent majority. As the most senior public servant in the Department of Indian Affairs, Duncan Scott, said it was to "kill the Indian in the child". It also killed the bond these children had with their parents or siblings and grandparents. When finally released from the claws of these psychos they did not know how to be husbands, wives, or parents themselves. Most of them resorted to drinking to drown their pain. We, human beings are bonkers!

Now that I have vented my political righteousness, it is time for me to explore what I can find out about the Prince Rupert seaport on the city library computers. It is apparently the closest and deepest year long open water seaport in North America to Asian ports, closer by one thousand nautical miles. It is connected to rail transport and can deliver goods up to a week faster than from any other western seaport on the continent to many major cities in Canada and the USA. Korea, China, and Taiwan load and unload their sea vessels in Prince Rupert. It can accommodate the largest vessels and is also a port of call to cruise ships on their way to and from Alaska. It is the end point of the inside passage through which these same cruise ships sail mostly from Seattle or Vancouver on their way to and from Alaska. I suppose, although it is not mentioned in the documentation, that like any port it must harbour some unsavoury characters. I have read somewhere that it is the choice point of entry for illegal human trafficking from Asia. Cynthia and Macky's Norwegian Ruby should soon dock in Prince Rupert if it has not already done so. Tomorrow I will stroll downtown to get a better feel of the city and see if I can get information on the ship's whereabouts.

For now as it is getting late I better return to my nest with the book I bought 'The First Nations of British Columbia' by Robert J. Muckle, on sale as a used discarded book from the library. For supper I got two granny smith apples, a bag of baby carrots a little container of Humus and I splurged on a can of readymade whipped cream. A Feast!

Sunday:

The motel is not busier than yesterday, just Harvey's truck. I suppose the clientele is mostly hunters and fishermen I saw a big freezer in the laundry room to store the catch.

In my room I spread my food, book, and glasses on the table, and I turn the TV on to listen to the news. I can only get four channels. The announcer says that the police are making progress but it is too early in the investigation to release sensitive information. The two politicians interviewed are outraged and promise tighter laws that will prevent anything of the sort from happening again. More policemen, tougher sentences. They also claim to mourn sincerely for the unfortunate victims and their families. A few people were stopped on the street to give their opinions. An older man deplores where the world is going to, that life was much simpler when he was young, a woman in her fifties is petrified on account of her teenage daughter wearing too much lipstick which attracts hoodlums and a young fellow is very happy that he does not have the means to eat in such a pricey restaurant. It is now the time for the weather conditions in the province and the sports news.

I try to switch to the Vancouver Chinese channel, not that I speak or understand Chinese, my total vocabulary in Mandarin is about one hundred words but that language fascinates me. I am trying to learn it so the news is a good start because at least for the most part I know what they are talking about since I just heard it a few minutes ago in English. I am training my ears to grasp the different inflections that still puzzle me. I learned that the simple word 'Ma' can mean at least five widely different concepts depending on how it is inflected? That is true of every single syllable. I read somewhere that if you know eight hundred characters in Chinese you will be able to read the newspaper. At the rate I am learning I will be one hundred and twenty before I can read the weather report. All this to say that one cannot get the Canadian Chinese channel in this motel but I can be treated to a Haïda celebration dance on the local channel. So I take my crossword puzzle book to bed and retire early. At three in the morning I am woken up by some fierce banging against the wall, some laughing and cursing. Harvey got himself at least two new happy clients in heat.

Monday:

After coffee this morning, I call Macky and Cynthia. Macky says he cannot talk right now but to call back in fifteen minutes. On my second call, I get Cynthia, who calls me Sweetie. In muffled tone she says she is very scared, that she does not leave the cabin because she is almost sure that she recognized the fellow who had come in the restaurant and was eyeing everyone before the shoot out. She says he is on the ship. She says now she wishes they had come with me to my "lovely cabin in the woods". I don't want to disappoint her about the cabin so I say nothing. I just listen. When she asks how I spend my days I explain that I am exploring the region. Most vacationers have gone home because school starts next week so it is very quiet in the parks and I can enjoy long walks in solitude. Today I am going to walk in Butze Rapids Park. She says that she loves nature. Didn't I notice the lovely flowers she has growing on her balcony? As if I had had the time or leisure to tour her apartment! She also says that she is a golfer and loves the green. Poor Cynthia she can be so out of it sometimes! I don't want her or Macky with me now; they would spoil my fun with their expectations of comfort and their fragile sense of dignity. I inquire about the possibility of having her meals brought up to her cabin to avoid any confrontations. She says that's what she has been doing. So she is safe for the moment.

Robin the Valiant

Once I hang up I stuff a bottle of water, an apple and half of my carrots in my packsack and I am off to the park. The entrance is a fifteen minute drive from the motel. According to the brochure there is a two mile, well-maintained, easy going trail through old growth forest, trekking across bogs, wetlands and swamps carpeted with moss. There is an outlook platform to view the rapids. Those are reversal tidal rapids best observed half an hour after high tide, the brochure also claims. That should be interesting to see if I calculate my timing properly.

As I thought it would be, the park is deserted. I will never tarry to be awed by the beauty of our planet. I read last month the amazing book by the physicist Brian Greene – The elegant Universe- where he talks about the eleven dimensions and I wonder, if we could glimpse or apprehend more dimensions than we do, would we also be able to perceive that much more beauty? I don't think I could survive it. The astronauts have returned to talk about the awe they felt in space that has changed their outlook on life. Life appears so easy, all you have to do is look, breathe and forget your petty problems, I feel like singing yet I don't dare lest I disturb the harmony. By gaining consciousness and the desire to conquer we have mostly lost the deep knowledge that we are an ever so tiny and yet so important part of the universe. The 'Me' disappears, all you have to do is let go, as all the truly inspired "advanced souls" will tell you, and a profound joy invades all your cells. Strange that I never could do that in any of the ashrams I haunted in my younger years. The fancy cross-legged positions, the chants, the beatings of cymbals or other torturing percussion instruments, the smell of incense, none of these devices work for me. I tried very hard in search of Wealth, Health and Happiness. I sang and danced Hare Krishna with shaven yellow robed dudes who had searched and found or said they had found, I sat for a fee at the feet of a black-bearded guru from Kazatstan or thereabouts drooling wisdom from his fat-lips in garbled English, I sang "Praise The Lord" in a spiritual church where a skimpy officiate with bulging eyes I had never met before called me Little Sister, nothing worked. I even studied numerology from a New Zealander who obviously had developed his art from counting sheep and that's when I met Edgar, my number one. Yet, ensconced in my favourite armchair, give me Mozart music, or a Monty Python production and I am off, rid of all my pain bodies as Eckhart Tolle calls your different blockages; I am at one with the universe, even the multi-verse as some new physicists like to call it, I experience what seems to me infinite space and freedom, I don't even feel my bunion anymore. Not that I want to be one of the blessed chosen, I enjoy too much all my emotions and my shortcomings, I love to immerse myself in them but it is also nice to know that there is another place where I can go and be free of all troubled waters. It makes me more resilient and in a sense more serene, even so, I tend to hide my "I" serenity.

I walk for an hour and a half in a semi-trance and now I sit on a bench for a drink of water and maybe have a bite. A young man is coming from the opposite direction. We make eye contact, he smiles at me and I smile at him. After a polite 'May I' he sits on the other end of the bench. I get a jolt; my pulse is beating so very fast, this fellow could be Edgar twenty five years ago. Same black soft curls, same almond shaped dark eyes, same long-fingered hands, same ease in the movement. He is dressed as a trekker. Nice new hiking boots, wide cotton pants, a rain jacket and a no-nonsense backpack from which he pulls out a thermos bottle. He takes a long sip.

"What a gorgeous place!", he says in a quiet voice.

"Yes, are you from around here?"

"No, as a matter of fact it is my first visit. A friend of mine has a cottage not far from here but since I am a bit early for our meeting I decided to explore the region a little. If all goes well I will be here very often from now on. What about you?"

"No, it is my second visit, but the first time I did not see too much." I am surely not going to tell him my story. "This time I am staying a while longer."

"Are you travelling alone? It could be dangerous you know all by yourself in the woods, I hear it is bear country. How long are you staying?"

"Another few days, I guess. I don't have any particular plans; it will depend on my cash."

"Where are you staying? If I may ask? Maybe we could go for walks together. I could come and pick you up I don't know anybody around here. I will be busy I imagine, but not so much that I can't afford a nice walk in a park."

"I don't see myself walking with you I could not keep your pace, but we could meet after our walks and shoot the breeze for a while sitting on a bench like today. That would be fine with me."

I said "Fine?"; I am thrilled down to the tip of my toes. I am in love at first sight again. A second Number One? What a fool I am at my age! I bet I fluttered my eyelids and he could be my son! Is there a way to be rid of these hormonal drives, or at least a graceful manner to handle them? I think of the lecherous Italian Premier Berlusconi in his seventies with his bunga-bunga parties and how the media derides him. Am I depraved?

"I am not such a fast walker I prefer to stroll leisurely and listen to the grass grow. I am not as young as all that."

"Now you are going to tell me you are eighty but you have an excellent plastic surgeon", I quip.

He laughs. "And you, you are very young for your age!" We both giggle and that cements our lasting friendship.

We exchange phone numbers and part after making sure we will meet again tomorrow at the same spot for two o'clock in the afternoon. This is Robin, what a lovely name! Back in my room I turn the clock-radio on and I dance to the tune of some rap music composed I swear by a teenage Inuit since I don't understand a word he says. There is a timid tap at the door. Could someone be annoyed by the noise?

It's a cute little Indian boy, not older than eight, with a small package. He says that Harvey, his Dad, told him to bring this over to the nice granny in number five and that his Dad is sorry about the noise last night. He tells me that it is Indian candy, meaning cured salmon with maple syrup. I had never tasted it but he is right, it's delicious.

I invite the boy in and we have a philosophical chat about school; and swimming and pestering little sisters while chewing Indian candy and baby carrots dipped into a splash of whipped cream from the can I had bought yesterday because I had finished my hummus last night. He is called Jeo, short for Jeopardy, the TV show, because his Dad wanted him to be smart, that's why he called him so.

"And are you?" I ask

He does not think so because he likes to close his eyes in class and the teacher thinks he is asleep and keeps sending notes to his parents who get mad at him.

"Are you really sleeping when you close your eyes?"

"No, I don't think so because behind my eyes I see and hear animal friends talking about things."

"What do they talk about?"

"They talk mostly about the moon changing everyday and sometimes hiding behind clouds to play. Sometimes me too, when my mother thinks I am sleeping in my room I look for the moon through the slates in the window and I talk to her." He also says that his friend from school has a granny who can take off her teeth whenever she wants to and drops them in a glass of water. He asks me if I can do it too. When I confess to my shame that I cannot, I feel that I drop down a notch from the esteem he had developed for me. You can't win them all. I love this place nonetheless, I should think of moving up here. In no time, I have made appealing, handsome friends. I would almost have forgotten the reason I am here if it had not been for Macky's cell phone ringing. I chime the friendliest "Hello" that I have uttered in the past four years.

Cynthia is talking in a hushed, altered voice. She is obviously distraught; maybe she lost her marbles at sea. She calls me Wilma and she says they need me urgently, that I should come and get them right away. Macky takes over, bless him, he says they are in Prince Rupert Harbour. I should decide immediately on an inconspicuous place to meet because he cannot talk very long, his cell phone will be out of batteries soon and he forgot to bring the plug to recharge it. I give them indication to meet at Tim Horton's. It's the only place I know and please don't dress fancy. That goes for the two of them. He understands. When it comes to certain things like that it is much easier for women to relate to homosexual men than to the testosterony types.

And I thought I was going to have a nice relaxing vacation!

Cynthia without her jewellery does not sparkle as much, she is very upset and Macky looks ten years older. He holds Cynthia's hand. They seem relieved to see me. She is certain she has recognized at least one of the gun men involved in the shooting as a passenger on the ship; she also thinks that he spotted her. I ask for more details but she is so beside herself with fear that I am not sure I can make much sense out of her. I have to get them out of here as soon as possible because in spite of them having dressed as I recommended her overall behaviour and the pricey luggage at their feet are going to make us noticeable. We are off to Harvey's paradise to further elaborate a plan of action. Macky is upset by the dusty look of his car. I drive. We are all silent in the car engrossed in our individual scenarios. I, wondering how they are going to react to my newly found Eden, Cynthia in the vacuum state of panic and Macky, judging from his dull look, regretting his hasty decision to help, wishing to withdraw gracefully from that big messy affair and wash his precious car. They are a big load on my shoulders. I wish I could dump them in a lake.

As I thought, they are not a bit impressed by my arrangement. I explain, they explain, I talk, they talk, I shout, Macky says he is going to the police. Cynthia and I scream. Harvey knocks on the door. He is worried, we all become civil again. I tell him that we found a spider in the closet. Macky rolls his eyes for Harvey's benefit - us guys let's be gentle with the little ladies. I tell Harvey I will soon come to see him. He leaves with a smile. Macky sits down and invites us to follow suit. He plays the role of the pacifier, the negotiator.

"Listen, if we don't work together in this situation, you girls will be in a lot of trouble. What I propose is that I drive back home, this is where I have all my valuable connections, I go to the police…"

We utter little shrieks politely.

"Hold it a minute! I won't tell them your names or where you are, I will just describe a hypothetical situation. And believe me I won't be talking with a constable, I will go much higher, to somebody who has chutzpah and discretion. He might be in a position to offer you protection."

We shriek some more but are still polite. Cynthia raises her hand like in kindergarten when you need to go, she has something to say. I hope that she wants to leave too. Macky, the magnanimous, gives her the floor. Her stiff upper lip has weakened some. Her lower jaw is quivering; she is on the verge of crying. She has lost her gumption that I enjoyed so much. I feel sad for her but mostly for myself. A potential friend is slipping away from me.

"You see, now the thing that has troubled me a lot for a day or two is that when I made the reservations at the restaurant I gave my last name and phone number which the maître d' must have written in the ledger. If the gangsters did not pick it up, the police surely did. So we are not only wanted by the gang but also by the police. I do not want to be a witness, even if the police find enough clues to apprehend the criminals, it might take months before they go to trial, I also think, as a matter of fact I am sure, that these people did not act on their own. They belong to a network of organized crime. I do believe that Clara and I are in more serious danger than we think. I feel much safer here; I do not want to go home just now." She regains some poise as she speaks. It makes me feel more confident to realize that Cynthia is still on the right track.

Macky seems relieved too. He has had enough adventure, I think. So we go to Harvey together to retain a room for the night for Macky who is going to leave with his precious "dusty" car early tomorrow morning but not before he drives us to a car rental office in town where Cynthia is going to get a car under my name. Macky will let us use his cell phone. We make a weak tea and retire soon after. Once alone with me since we are sharing the room at her request Cynthia whispers in my ear that she will tell me more when Macky is gone. She fears that the walls are too thin to secure privacy.

Tuesday:

It is morning, Cynthia is chirping, she says that it would not take much to make this lovely room a bit more cheerful. Flowers maybe and definitely a nicer bedspread. She sings "My darling Clementine" again. I wish she would have a wider repertoire in music. I am in a good mood too because I have a date with Robin. I am not sure how I am going to wiggle my way out of Cynthia's clutches but I know I am going to find a way. I don't want her to know about him. I must fear competition.

We go out for breakfast, the three of us; Macky pays for the car with his credit card, Cynthia reimburses him with a cheque. The car is rented under my name. We are so clever. After tender advice from both sides, "Be careful on the road", "Stay clear of trouble", etc... Macky leaves. Cynthia wants to go shopping. She is looking for good Earl Gray tea, fruits, enough vegetables to make several monstrous salads, and smoked salmon. True to herself she also buys a bunch of artificial flowers and a vase.

On the way back to the motel, she tells me that Macky is an incorrigible flirt, and that he had an eye on the fellow she recognized as one of the baddies from the restaurant. That's why she was so upset fearing that he would talk too much. They had an argument about it on the ship. She is sure the fellow played him to get to her but he would not hear it. He is sure that he is still a very attractive man, a catch if you would but underneath he is very insecure. I listen still trying to figure out how I am going to present the fact to Cynthia that I will be leaving her for a while. I gently dissert on my need to be alone from time to time. She understands, she says she has a good feeling about the two of us and that we should feel free to follow our inclinations. She is going to be busy rearranging the room and that she wants to talk with "Dear" Harvey. So I leave for the park with her blessings. I suspect that she is going to take a nap because for the last two days she has not slept very well and she does look tired. It seems to me that all her bubbling is a put-on, deep-down she is a lonely person craving for love. She had me fooled for a while. I will try to come back as soon as I can.

More mishaps

I spot only two cars in the parking lot. That's two more than yesterday at about the same time. I start my walk at a leisurely pace but I am very excited to learn more about handsome Robin. I wonder if one of the cars in the parking lot is his. After an hour of enjoying the lovely trail without meeting a soul I reach the bench where I rested the day before. I hum quietly to myself some old folksong from my childhood. Robin must have been busy, or he forgot all about me. I will wait a while and go back to Cynthia. Birds are chirping; one can hear the rushing water in the rapids. How relaxing! I will come back tomorrow even if Robin does not show up, after all this might be my last true vacation, I better take full advantage of it but I feel a bit let down by Robin.

It is strange. One of the bird chirping sounds like he is singing my name. I turn my head in the direction of the sound and I spot what looks like a human hand moving from behind a tree trunk. I am a little scared. I hastily gather my bag and start in the direction of the parking lot at a brisk pace. I am sure someone is following me.

"Keep walking!" a voice whispers. I am not sure it is Robin's voice. I am that stupid to have implicitly trusted a young man I had never met before?

"Don't run, make as little noise as possible, once in your car drive towards town, if all goes well I will meet you in an hour at the library. Lock your car. I am following you. When you reach the parking lot check first for anyone nearby including me. Stay hidden until the path is clear. Hurry!"

Now I am almost sure it is Robin talking. He must have spotted a bear or a cougar. What a chivalrous escort! If he had not scared me so much with his silly whispering I would run to him and kiss him.

The path seems endless now, I stumble a few times over a rock, I lose my bag of food but I am approaching the parking. I must have twisted my ankle in the haste because it hurts like hell. Noiselessly someone grabs my arm from behind and puts his hand forcefully over my mouth making me swallow my scream down my throat. I am being carried behind a tree. I try to bite the hand and then I hear male voices getting closer. We are not alone, my abductor and I. With a knock behind my knees I am made to drop on all fours. I can hardly breathe. Robin, for I am sure now it is him, is holding me too tight around the middle. I must concentrate on something other than my fear to regain my composure. I don't know the appropriate composure one should adopt, squatting in the dirt with a big guy hugging you from behind, but I try my very best. For some reason I close my left eye, a blade of grass is tickling my nostril. My nose is squeezed against the bark of the tree. I have never looked at a tree trunk from so close through my right eye or my left eye for that matter. Two ants are dutifully hurrying up. A car is arriving or leaving then it is quiet again, the birds are resuming their conversations and Robin sets me free. I sneeze spraying my spit all over the ants; the ravens start a raucous protest from the trees nearby.

"We will wait another fifteen minutes and then you go." He hushes, "I will follow a bit later and we will meet at the library. Be very cautious, these people are killers. They just popped two guys I knew, or at least that I had met. I will try to tell you the little I know in a while, where it is safer." With that he disappears noiselessly through the woods.

Before I get in my car I take a good look at the one remaining car in the lot since it must be Robin's, I hope I will remember the first numbers of the license plate. When it comes to cars I am a complete idiot. For me a car has a color, four wheels and a license plate.

I should stop over at the motel to check on Cynthia but if I do I am not sure I can tell her what happened, it might throw her again in a loop of panic. I had left Macky's cell phone with her so I will call her from the library to give some excuses for my lateness. I am afraid I have turned into an angel of death since I met the cat. I have read somewhere that there are no coincidences. If so, all that is happening must have a connecting thread but am I equipped to unravel it? After living an uneventful life of routines for so many years my mind is full of spider webs. At least Edgar used to keep me on my toes. How I still miss him!

Aside from the librarian reading, the library is unoccupied. She lifts her head and smiles at me. She seems to recognize me from my last visit. I go to the newspapers section because this is how I remember that spies and private detectives do it on TV. They hide behind a newspaper and make a little hole in the middle to survey the comings and goings in hotel lobbies. The librarian is watching me so I cannot cut a hole and worse she is approaching with a kind grin on her face. She wants to talk and I don't; I need some quiet time to assess my situation. I read that the police are still searching for the perpetrators of the massacre in the downtown restaurant but they now have several interesting leads. It is not from Macky for he is still on the road; at best he will be back in town tomorrow evening and won't talk to the police till the day after.

What if Robin is leading me on? Two dead he said. How did he find out? Why was he trying to protect me and from what or whom? As I am pondering I see him stride leisurely through the science fiction alley, answering courteously to the librarian's anxious desire to help. She then scurries to find whatever he asked for. Turning in my direction he drops a note on my lap without even a glance at me.

We are co-conspirators and I like that. I am living an adventure that gets my heart pumping with excitement.

The note says: "If you think your motel is a safe place, leave now and I will follow you." I do not want to share Robin's attention with Cynthia so I stay put with the newspaper glued to my nose and now I hear Cynthia's voice, I peek over the paper, she is talking to the librarian, little shy Jeo at her heels. To my dismay he comes directly towards me and sits on the next chair.

"Hi, Granny Clara, I saw your shoes." He says with a wide smile.

"How did you know it was me?"

"You are the only person I know who has a green lace on only one of her shoes."

Well, this is not a date, it's a convention!

"How did you get here with Cynthia? I have the car."

"My Dad drove us. Mrs. Cynthia wants me to read books."

Busybody Cynthia has been on a rampage again. She is now coming to meet me all smiles.

"I had an intuition I would see you at the library. How are you MyDear? I am having a lovely time with Jeo and Harvey. We are looking for good books for Jeo who should do well in school so he can become an important person in his tribe."

Robin is stepping in with a book in his hand greeting me very civilly. I introduce him as a reader who recommended a book. He hands me the book "Understanding Chinese for Idiots" by Olaf Vitollini, possibly a descendant of Marco Polo. I thank him with a wink.

"We will get a nice book for Jeo, the boy needs to read, go get something nice for tea and we will all have refreshments at the motel" she asserts, turns to Robin and invites him too.

At the motel, I must admit the room, is more cheerful. There is a tablecloth spread on the table and fresh flowers in a glass. Cynthia sparkles. "That outing did not do much for you, you look dusty and out of sorts MyDear, maybe you could refresh yourself while

I am preparing tea and in the meantime Mr. Robin can tell me all about himself."

Robin looks puzzled, Jeo is leafing through the Chinese book, Cynthia tells him to go get his mother because she wants to learn more about that gorgeous recipe with fresh salmon and dandelion leaves. How am I going to get to talk alone with Robin? After asking for a phone number where he can reach us, and thanking us profusely for the best cup of tea he has had in a long time, he makes his way out but not before Cynthia bids him to call her, should he happen to be in town, and she gives him her address and phone number at home. I am seething as I accompany him to his car.

"Listen, I looked at the map and there is another park southeast of here on the Yellowhead Highway, Diana Lake. It should take you around half an hour to reach. I am almost sure it will be safe to meet there tomorrow, let's try for one in the afternoon. I really need to talk to you alone. I must leave I have an urgent appointment. Wish me luck. You friend is delightful but you are the one I want to talk to." He says with a conspirator undertone.

I am so pleased that I feel like kissing him again but Cynthia and Jeo are at the window watching and I don't want to spoil my secret delight by having to explain my deportment. So I give him a non-committal wave and shout: "Thank you for the book." as he revs his car out of the parking lot. I don't know what is that attraction one gets at the first sight of a particular individual. With Robin it is as if I have known him for ever. Like some seer I once met would probably say, it might be an acquaintance from another life if you believe in reincarnation.

I have until tomorrow morning to find an alibi to get away from Cynthia for a few hours. As I get back to the suite I am told that we have been invited for supper by Harvey's wife and Cynthia is exploring her suitcase for something appropriate to wear. I recommend jeans and a tee-shirt but she is not convinced. She says that to honour the host she should dress her best and I hope that the sense of decorum among the people of the Northwest Coast has some remnants of existence in Harvey's family. We will both bring little gifts of appreciation.

Macky calls, he says that he has decided to get back on board the ship and he has arranged for his car to be driven to town by next week. He sounds very happy but is concerned for our welfare. We do our best to reassure him. He also tells Cynthia that she should feel free to use his apartment while he is away. She hangs up in a very agitated way. She paces the room calling him a turn-coat, a flirt, a low-life, and chokes on "bastard". Now her lipstick is all crooked and her mascara is spread over her cheeks. In the condition she is in I don't think I should tell her. I just advise for two or three deep breaths before marching to Harvey's and hand her a Kleenex. She looks a bit like one of those masks I saw displayed in the museum of anthropology. It's the first time I see her in a snit, behind that mask of jolliness she also has a temper that makes me feel more comfortable. I have seen her scared even panicky, conniving, lady-like, affectionate with the cat, but the fact that she can get loose on anger and frustration is a bonus in our situation. Anger, as two-bit psychologists will say, is a great motivator, a booster of energy. I often use it to propel myself into action. I love negative feelings, like having prickling itches to scratch, spit, kick, insult, or fart in someone's face, all this is awakening my senses, I feel my blood pumping from head to toes. I am alive; it's almost as exhilarating as being in love and not a bad substitute. Maybe this is why so many old people are cranky since they have dried out their potential for love and sex. For upliftment or loosening their arthritic moods they can only resort to choleric fits.

June, Harvey's wife is hiding her wisdom behind a shy smile. She looks very young. The house is the way I like them, messy. The children are very convivial and not intimidated in the least. Jeo is my pal and makes sure everyone acknowledges it. The little girl is fascinated by Cynthia's jewellery. The food is served in clean disparate slightly chipped crockery but tasty and plentiful. Cynthia liberally sprinkles her conversation with words like "gorgeous", "marvellous", "adorable" and so on. She seems to have recovered from her foul mood; it could be she was hungry. Nobody but Jeo notices her crooked lipstick, he tells me in confidence that he thinks she must have taken a bad licking and he feels a bit sorry for her. In a sense he is right. It would take too long to correct his inkling so I leave it at that.

I inquire about June and Harvey's family. They both have brothers and sisters living in the area. No, they don't speak the original language of their people, very few people still do. No, they did not go to residential schools but their parents did with disastrous results. They were released from the ordeal ashamed of their origins and inveterate alcoholics. Harvey and June, having experienced firsthand the ravages alcohol can cause, have vouched never to touch it whatever the temptation. They say that they are not alone in this case and that slowly you can see a new pride and sense of direction emerging among their peers. A cousin of theirs is a lawyer, another is studying in university to become an anthropologist, and another one is a full-fledged nurse in a big hospital. They like the motel because it resembles the long cedar houses of yore. Also it makes them meet nice people and although it does not bring much in money it makes enough to feed the family.

Back in our room, Cynthia has nothing but praises for the family, the food, the ambiance, etc. and rattles off a string of all the superlative adjectives of appreciation in her vocabulary. She stumbles a bit on some of the most difficult ones but it does not matter. I am dreaming of a scheme to free myself for a few hours tomorrow to meet Robin. Before turning in, dolled up in pink sateen pj's, and her face all creamed up, she says that the one thing she did not understand is why they looked so upset about boarding school. After all that's where they were taught English, the true language of the country they live in. I am too tired to elaborate or even to get incensed. She shuts her eyes on the last word:"Thank Winston "MyDear" we found each other!"

"Hummm…"

Macky, the flirt gets it

The phone rings after breakfast, Cynthia takes it.

"No, you must have the wrong number. Who is calling, please? Just a second." And she hands me the phone.

"It's the hospital calling", a male voice says.

"It's about Mr. Fairmount. Mr. Malcolm Fairmount."

"Yessssss"

"There has been an accident. I am calling on his behalf. He can't talk at the moment. I am just relaying a message to his friend Wilma. Are you Wilma?"

"Yesssss"

Probably hearing my hesitations and total lack of enthusiasm, he concludes:"Well, if you care for him you can come anytime to the hospital, room 204." He hangs up.

Is this an ambush? Has big mouth Macky talked? The phone number is a local one. I go to see Harvey telling him that since Cynthia has lost her purse someone she does not know keeps phoning, scaring her. He says that now it explains why someone like her would stay at his motel. He had been wondering if she was in hiding. Not dumb this Harvey. He confirms that the call came from the hospital and offers to go and see for himself since he was going to town anyway. We will follow him and wait outside the hospital until he comes back with more information. Jeo is coming along too; he has to buy some school stuff.

We are waiting in the car in the hospital parking lot. Cynthia is most agitated. She wrings her hands, huffs and puffs as I start to search for a paper bag in case she hyperventilates. All of a sudden she laughs and embraces me sidewise.

"What silly geese we are!" she exclaims "The fellow on the phone asked for Wilma. Do you see? Wilma, that's a code name that only the three of us know. If he used it it's because he wanted us to be cautious."

She is right. I too feel relieved. Jeo who is sitting in the back of the car waiting for his father taps on my shoulder.

"What's a code name?" he asks.

"Oh, that's a secret name you give someone when you don't want other people to know whom you are talking about. You see, Malcolm is my big brother and when he was angry with me when we were children; that's how he called me so our mother would not know he was bad-mouthing me."

"Oh, that is a good idea! I am going to call my little sister: "Turnip", from now on whenever I feel like kicking her."

"You don't like turnips?"

"No, I don't like veggies especially when they are called turnips. But you said that Mr. Malcolm is your big brother, why do you look old and he does not so much?"

"It's because he always ate all his veggies and I didn't."

"You know, Granny Clara, there was a man who came to the motel once, he said he was a muscle-man, he ate lots of veggies but he was much smaller than Dad and he had a beard."

"Maybe he was short but very strong."

"I don't think so. He did not speak English very well. He said he was a French speaking muscle-man. That's why he had to kneel on a small carpet and touch the floor with his head four times a day. I used to look at him from our kitchen window, because I want to be a muscle-man too so I can lick big Jeff in grade five who is always making fun of me in the school bus."

"I get it", I exclaim, "You said this man spoke French so he probably said He was a 'Musulman', tried to pronounce it the English way and it came out as 'Mussel-mane' when he meant Moslem which is a religion."

"Grandpa says that religion is a dirty word that makes you dumb."

"Your Grandpa is a wise man even if he is not a 'muscle man'."

"I like you Granny Clara; you are cool as a cucumber like Daddy says."

"What else does your Daddy say about us?"

"He says that you are a child of the Raven, like we are. But you are in disguise with a different skin color and that I have to be extra polite with Mrs. Cynthia because she is sad and that's why she has to wear all the jewellery to make her shine from the outside."

Cynthia, who had been quiet during all this conversation, exhales loudly as if she had been punched in the stomach. She pulls out a handkerchief and wipes her eyes. She is sobbing noiselessly and I hug her tightly.

Harvey is back, he tells us that the road is clear. He identified Macky and we should brace ourselves because he does not look his best. He leaves with Jeo the little tattle-tale.

In the ward we peek through the glass pane of room 204. Macky's left arm is in a sling, one eye completely shut with ugly puffed up black, red and blue surroundings, and as he smiles I notice some front teeth missing. The nurse at the station tells us he also has two broken ribs and has been sedated because he suffers a lot and has trouble breathing causing him to panic. She says that he cannot talk much at the moment. He has been airlifted from a cruiser this morning. The police have been notified. Apparently from the report he was found by a steward unconscious in his cabin. Cynthia cries openly. I feel really sorry for him. A nice police officer comes in, pad and pen at the ready.

"This is clearly a case of aggression. We need to know more about the victim. The ship's security team is investigating too. But since he has been transferred here as an emergency we also need to prepare a file on him. I am going to ask you a few questions." I don't know about Cynthia but I start feeling very uneasy.

"First, which one of you is Wilma?" We both point at each other.

"Wilma is his cat." I assert with a nervous laugh. Cynthia nods vigorously.

"So, you mean to say that he called his cat when he found himself in the hospital?" asks the facetious police officer.

"Well you see, that cat is our cat really but Macky thinks that we act so much like the cat that he calls us Wilma too." I reply rather astutely. Cynthia is nodding so hard that I fear her head is going to fall off.

"So which one of you, "Wilmas", is related to Mr. Fairmount?" says the officer with what I detect as a glint of doubt in her eyes.

"Neither, we are neighbours, that's all and we share a cat."

"And what are you doing in Prince Rupert? Because I assume you both live in Vancouver since you are telling me that you are neighbours and Mr. Fairmount's address is in Vancouver."

Cynthia and I are holding hands peevishly like two schoolgirls caught by the principal while writing "We hate fuckin Geografie end Mrs Cornell and Luba gikorski" signs all over the walls of the toilets. Something I actually did in grade three with my best friend at the time. We got three weeks detention under Mrs. Cornell's supervision. We were as innocent then as Cynthia and I are now.

All at once Cynthia lets go of my hand, straightens up and commands with an authoritative voice, "Look here, Officer, are we suspects in this affair? We do not, and I repeat, do not tolerate to be interrogated in such a way. Dear Mr. Fairmount was on a ship when this terrible accident occurred, so obviously we were not the ones who beat him up. What seems important to me is to find out who did. I understand it is your job; but remember we can't help you there. We are in this lovely part of the world for our enjoyment, a vacation, you might say. Right now we want to be with our poor dear friend who suffered terrible injuries. We have no idea what happened to him nor how." And with that she steps towards Macky's room.

The officer, a young woman, is somewhat taken aback by Cynthia's outburst. She smiles at me.

"Sorry, I did not mean to be accusing or anything of the sort, I have been sent to write a report and Mr. Fairmount is not making much sense right now. I don't know what the doctors gave him but he laughs and cries at the same time. All he was able to produce was a phone number that is registered under his name; yet it's one of you two who answered, I thought I could gather some information from you. Sorry again if I offended you."

By the time she finishes her apologies I have regained my composure, good old Cynthia did it again she saved the day down talking the over confident policewoman with her uppity veneer. I am safe giving my name for the police have no record of me implicated in any of the crimes committed lately or at any time for that matter.

"Mr. Fairmount and I have been good friends for some times now. When he decided to take a cruise to Alaska I thought it would be fun for me to come to Prince Rupert for a little vacation since I could not afford the cruise. He let me have one of his cell phones since I don't have one of my own and he had two, so we could keep in touch. He was worried about me alone in unknown territories."

"But we have the list of the passengers on the ship and we know he was accompanied on this trip by a lady."

"Yes Cynthia, but she did not like the ship and when they docked in Prince Rupert she preferred to stay with me. So Macky, I mean Mr. Fairmount sailed alone from there on."

"Would you know if he had any other acquaintances on board?"

"None whatsoever. You will excuse me, I am still under the shock of what happened to him but if I can be of any more help I will be happy to answer your questions tomorrow. For now I want to go see him and comfort my friend."

The policewoman leaves not before handing me her card.

Macky who had been faking temporary disorientation is himself although in a lot of pain. He says that he did not swallow all the pills he has been given because he did not want to lose his wits before talking to us. He is now even more convinced that we are in real danger. The fellow he had a romantic eye on, and that he had invited for supper in his cabin was mostly interested in Cynthia.

"He is sure that we are a couple and that I play on the side, he wanted to know where you were, Cynthia. I never told him anything even when he started hitting me. At first, he only slapped me but then he became very violent, called me a pervert, and I fainted I think. I don't recall him breaking my arm or my ribs. Do I look that bad? Nobody wants to bring me a mirror. I hate these hospital gowns they are very unbecoming. I must look like a big splash of vomit." He cries. He wants to fly directly back home with Cynthia. He says that he feels isolated here; he misses his own network of friends, his doctor, his things. Cynthia could stay with him in his apartment until the big search is over and the hoodlums are in jail. He does not mention me.

Cynthia is hyperventilating again. I look for a nurse or a paper bag. The nurse calls a doctor and they administer her a dose of tranquilizer. She is out. I tell the nurse I have an urgent errand to do and I will be back by four this afternoon. No excuses, no lies needed, I am off to meet Robin. I need to detach myself from all this pathos, this fear. The not-knowing is getting to me too. What else am I going to discover that I don't want to know?

Robin's story

Alone at last! First I must cool down; these two fools have gotten me on edge. Driving on a beautiful empty road relaxes me. I start humming softly at first and now I am belting out the most idiotic songs I know. Somehow my head gets clearer when I do that. Maybe that is how the black people of the Deep South used to do it and still do to return to a quieter mood after all the abuse they had to endure. I should start a screaming club with the sole purpose to belt out one's worries; I would be sparing on the Halleluiahs though.

I am a bit early for my date with Robin, so I stop at a gas station for a drink; the cashier looks at me and smiles. I look at myself in a mirror behind the cash register. My hair is in total disarray, I look crazy and that is not good. I want to blend in with the scenery. I don't want to be identified.

Once I return to the car, I count the money I have left. Two hundred and twenty six dollars plus a few coins. I have not spent any of my monthly pension cheque, so it is not too bad as long as I remain careful. What if these two fly back to town and leave me stranded here? I don't even have enough to get back home. In some way I am less in danger than Cynthia because I don't think that either the gangsters or the police know my name or my address. Maybe I should try to make myself indispensable to Cynthia so she would pay for my return trip. Once back I could always forget about her if she rubs me the wrong way. I would still have to teach her another song; I am getting pretty tired of "Dear Clementine".

I could also drop dead, at my age it is a common thing to do and then all my problems would be solved. I listen to my heart; the old thing is ticking faithfully, but you never know. Cynthia could conk out too; hopefully not before we return safely home. And to think it all started with the blasted cat! Death is in the air around us. What about the twelve much younger people in the restaurant and now according to Robin these other two in the park?

Thinking of Robin, why should I bother pursuing him? *"Now Clara, try to think straight for a moment because there is still time for you to turn around; try to convince Cynthia that she needs you and have her pay for the trip back home."* With me it is always a question of money, I am a prisoner of my own financial situation. I thought I had passed this stage; that I had reached a level of contentment within my means. I don't owe a cent to anyone anymore. I survive reasonably well with the pension I get. I am lucky to be healthy, to enjoy activities that don't cost anything like reading books that I can borrow free at the library a few blocks away from where I live; I have my computer that provides hours of entertainment and keeps me in touch with the world around me, my city is beautiful with lots of opportunities for delightful walks and to meet people. I enjoy talking with strangers, what I don't feel the need for is what people commonly refer to as friendship. "Friends" don't only want to unload their hang-ups on you like the anxiety of the removal of their gall bladder or other malfunctioning organ but they also want you to feel for them, to show them compassion, to comfort them, and to admit that due to an inclement fate they are the sufferers and you are the lucky one. "Friends" are seldom interested by your own questionings or drama which they deem futile compared to their personal struggles to survive. I don't like "Friends".

"So, Clara, why didn't you send Cynthia packing with her pricey cat?"
"Because I liked the idea of the nice meal she was offering."

"Clara, you are full of shit. You were bored and you wanted some entertainment at her expense. You are a selfish leech."

"She was bored too, otherwise she would not have invited me; she would have handed me five bucks for my trouble; and after all I did listen politely to her bloody inane stories."

"I don't want to talk about it anymore. I am on my way to meet the fellow of my dreams. Tra la laaa"

Sometimes the five cent psychologist imbedded in the recesses of my brain can be very aggressive. I wish I could have it extracted like you'd do a clogged up gall bladder or a rotten tooth. All these cogitations have brought me to the park entrance where I am supposed to meet Robin. I can see his car.

As we meet between the two cars, Robin gives me a big bear hug, and I melt in his arms.

"I was a bit scared that you wouldn't show up", he says with a big smile, "your friend seems to be very needy; you make an odd couple. Have you known each other long?"

"No as a matter of fact, I met her only two weeks ago. But that's a long story however short time wise. I'd rather talk about you. What are you doing in these parts of the world? Who are you? It's as if I have known you all my life and yet I know nothing about you."

"Alright, first my name is Robin Bullock. Well this is the name the dude who married my mother gave me when he adopted me. I was lucky enough that he split when I was around six. I was very scared of him. He used to slap me whenever he felt like it. If I cried he said I was a sissy and that he only meant it as a joke. He would do it in front of his friends to show what a good affectionate father he was. He wanted to raise me as a tough guy or so he said. One time I told him that when I became a real toughie I would kill him. He laughed so hard but when he looked at my eyes he knew I meant it. Fortunately for me he left us, my mother and me. My mother worked at all kinds of jobs that she mostly hated. She passed away last year. That was a big shock to me; I loved her.

She was sick in hospital for a good six months before that. At that time I was in third year university studying botany with a full scholarship. My grades deteriorated during her sickness, I lost the scholarship. I tried selling weed for an income; I was busted. I did three months only because it was a first offense. In jail I met a guy who gave me a name and phone number for when I got out. He assured me that this man could help me find a job."

We are walking side by side down a lovely nature path; I am listening. He seems to try to exorcise a huge dark cloud off his mind. I don't understand why he chose me as his confidant but I dare not interrupt him. He stops talking as if weighing whether he should go on. There is an aura of discomfort and perhaps even fear surrounding him. It might be safer for him if we'd go back to his childhood.

"You say that you don't like your name, which name would you rather adopt?" I ask in as jovial a tone as I can emit.

"Heath, my mother's name, because she is the one who raised me. Her name was Lucy Heath."

"What about your biological father, did you ever meet him?"

"Yes, my mother told me it was Uncle Ed."

I sense that we are on safer ground, Robin is relaxing a bit. We sit on a bench; he takes a deep breath and smiles.

"It feels so good to be with you! I haven't been myself since my mother died." He hugs me tight. I am putty in this boy-man's arms.

"Tell me more about this Uncle Ed of yours. Did you like him? Was he kind to you and your mother?"

"He was a fun guy, he always brought little gifts and I think he gave some money to my mother to help pay for the rent or whatnot. He would take me once in a while to a park. Once when I did not know yet that he was my real father, I asked him to be my father for real. He said that we should leave it at that, good friends, Uncle Ed. He said that fatherhood was grossly overrated. He said that I was a very lucky guy to have at least a loving mother. He also said that he felt lucky because he never met his own father. I asked my mother why she did not marry him, and she said that he was a nice guy but a bum. That you could not depend on him, that it would have been like having a second child and she could not afford that.

He never told us where he lived, or what he did for a living. The last time I saw him, I was around fifteen I remember because he was in the best of moods; he told us that our worries were over that he had hit it big. He gave two hundred dollars to my mother and some pretty candles. Then he disappeared we never saw him again."

I dare not ask but I must. My heart is playing havoc against my ribs. I hope I won't faint because now I recognize him. Robin is the boy on the picture I found in Edgar's wallet. I must not show him my distress. I feel like running but my legs would not carry me.

"Do you know Uncle Ed's last name?" I whisper.

"Yes, my mother told me just before she died. Ed Vittorio."

Now I asked. Stupid me! Edgar, you sneak, you white-bellied scum, you miserable bastard! You two-faced clown! I have been abused. I have been lied to... I must compose myself.

"And why were you so anxious to talk to me, a perfect stranger who only happens to like trekking down nature paths like you do?", I bleat hesitantly; I need to know if he knew of my existence. I am not going to ask for his date of birth. I can't, just in case he was born after I met Edgar which would confirm how I was maligned. It would not be out of character for my Edgar to cop out of the responsibilities of fatherhood. He had told me that he did not want children. It was fine with me since I was barren. I was in my early thirties then and I had made peace with the fact. I did not want to adopt either. Instead I supported girl's soccer teams, science projects, and lots of charitable organizations that dealt with the betterment of girls. I am engrossed in the 'Then' while my 'Now' is completely out of whack.

We have been very quiet for a spell, the two of us, I guess, mulling over our own drama. Then Robin looks like he made a decision, he turns, looks at me straight in the eye:

"I have been very lonely without my mother, she was my anchor and when I met you I had the feeling that I could talk to you, you look like a kind woman and an intelligent one. My girlfriend left me. She decided that I was too boring. She is right and I am a loser too. I am so scared but you see I am also afraid that if I told you I would put you in grave danger"

I know that I should say:"Don't tell me, then "and leave; but what is it? Empathy, curiosity, insane nosiness?

I blurt in what might be a motherly tone; Edgar's son, although I will never tell him, is a little bit my son after all, motherhood can be offered in all kinds of forms:"At my age, very little fazes me, if it can help you I am prepared to listen." But I must admit I am a little apprehensive, since I met that darned cat I have been on a disastrous roller coaster ride and I have met crazier people and situations than I have in the past fifteen years of my life. I also must remember never to tell him my last name. Fancy that, experiencing parenthood in my seventies!

"After my release from jail, I was flat broke, I had to sell my old motorcycle to pay the rent for the apartment we shared with my mother, I looked for jobs, I wrote probably one hundred applications. All I could find were minimum wage part-time dumb jobs. Then I remembered that phone number that fellow convict had given me. I phoned and got an appointment. The man I met, Tony, grilled me, it was exciting because he was mostly interested in my studies in botany. He also asked me if I could live rough and if I minded being isolated. He said that I would need a car and since I had no means of transportation, he offered me the use of one. The car I am using now."

He stops talking. I smell a rat.

"Are you bored? You are sure you want to know the rest?" he begs.

"You might as well get it off your chest."

"Do you know what bubble hash is?

"I know what hashish is because my late husband shared some with me from time to time but I don't have the means to indulge and even so I don't think I would if I could. Too much hassle, if you buy it on the street you don't know what kind you buy and I understand there is a lot of crap on the market."

"Bubble hash is relatively new. It is processed from cannabis using ice water. If it is well done, using plants that were not sprayed with insecticide, it contains up to 60 percent of cannabinoid, the stuff that gets you high as opposed to marijuana with 20 percent."

"Why are you telling me all this? Are you involved in this?"

"Up to recently, I smoked the occasional joint with friends, but as I was telling you, when I met this man that my friend in jail told me to contact I got a lot more involved."

"You are scaring me."

"You must understand, there are all kinds of people dealing with marijuana, but for the common misinformed people they are all criminals. As a matter of fact they are, since growing and exploiting the plant is illegal in most countries. So it is true that you will find some very shady even dangerous people involved in the trade but there are also some courageous individuals who sponsor the use of marijuana for what it is, a marvellous gift from nature that can provide remedies for many ailments, the seeds and oil extracted from it are excellent nourishment rich in essential fatty acids. Its fibres can be used to build sturdy housing at a fraction of the cost without depleting our forests; and so what if it can give you a high when you smoke it, what about alcohol or happy pills.

"Anyway it is in this spirit that I was hired to produce bubble hash for Tony who impressed me as a reasonable man with the wish to produce good quality rather than harmful junk."

"So far so good, I can hear the botanist in you, it is really too bad that you could not continue your studies." I say in a soothing tone.

Robin looks dejected, I feel he has more to say, yet does not know how to go on with his story. As for myself I am not sure I want to hear what will follow. It is starting to rain and I could use that as an excuse to run. He looks at me with pleading eyes. I am getting on the defensive. Who does this young fellow think I am to unload his dilemmas on me? And what do I care about marijuana or cannabis, as he calls it, I don't indulge in the junk? No, I must look after myself otherwise who will. It is pouring rain now and I trot back to the car. He follows, protecting me under the side of his jacket. I huff and I puff and there he is easing quietly on the passenger seat. If I had the strength I would push him out. We sit silently watching the big drops of rain splatter on the windshield. There is some rumbling of thunder coming from the mountains. I shiver. He takes off his jacket and wraps it around me. It is a little gesture, but how long has it been since someone has shown such delicate attention towards me? He fumbles in his backpack, finds his thermos bottle and pours me a warm cup of coffee. Just what I needed.

"Do you read the paper?" he inquires.

"I get it delivered"

"Then you could not miss it, it was on the front page a week ago, a horrible massacre in a restaurant downtown."

I almost drop my cup of coffee. "Oh, yes I saw that." I say dipping my nose in the cup while holding it as tight as I can to stop my hand from shaking. I better not open my mouth and just let it ride.

"Three psychos were responsible for that and two of them are lying dead in the park where we were yesterday." He whispers.

That is good news for me and even better for Cynthia. I am breathing better now.

"And how does that affect you outside of the fact that you were in the park when it happened? I don't understand."

"You see, Clara, I am almost sure that Tony, the fellow I work for, has something to do with that."

"What do you mean?"

"When I arrived at the cabin where I am supposed to work, two guys were just leaving, the same two guys I saw in the park and who left before us."

"Are you sure?"

"Positive. Tony was in the cabin when I came in. So they must have been talking to him"

"Let's not jump the gun, this Tony you are referring to might not have anything to do with the murders."

I know I wished for some excitement in my life, but this is clearly over my head. I am in the turmoil of dangerous and unknown waters. This Robin might be a lunatic even if he does not look like one. Robin might also be hallucinating, maybe he took too much of that stuff he is concocting. I must tiptoe through all this madness and return to my books on quantum physics and my cat food diet as soon as possible. Now what was the plan? To try to convince Cynthia to fork out for the trip back to town and dump all these crackpots as soon as possible. Action! I turn on the car ignition key. I am on my way. To hell with excitement!

I say with a smile, "Sorry, I have a friend in the hospital and I promised I would be back soon. So I must leave. I hope for your sake that you are making a mistake about your boss." Robin steps out of the car. He looks totally lost and pleads: "When will I see you again?" I don't answer.

Now driving I scream to the wind all the expletives of my extensive vocabulary. This is what cars are good for. I can't scream in my apartment, I can't scream while in public transport or on my walks without penalties, but in a car it is different. I pity people in countries where cars are at a premium. I wonder what they do to let off steam. Maybe that's why they make revolutions to voice loud and clear all their frustrations. Come to think of it, I should save a little every month just in order to be able to rent a car once in a while to do just that, shout. At least while I am still able to drive because I am getting on, age-wise I mean.

I feel a bit better now that I have exhausted my plethora of curses; I feel less like a loser. I start rewinding all I heard from Robin the dope. It's a thing with me; I always fall for fellows with curly black hair, olive skin and languid eyes. I imagine them serenading under my balcony and I get the hots. But at my age! *"Oh, well*

Clara, you will never learn and you will die a fool." You know what? I would not want me any other way. Better that than being a dried-up, sexless old sourpuss biddy. I still can't get over the fact that blasted Edgar never told me about Robin. Worse, I will never forgive him for offering MY CANDLES to his former girlfriend, shameless cad! No decency.

"Take it easy, Clara, the past is the past. You are supposed to be in the Now, Remember?" Then I get a flash. Did wimpy Robin actually use the words: cabin and Tony? I slam on the brakes in the middle of the fortunately traffic-free road; do a U-turn and pass Robin's car two minutes later; slam on the brakes again, U-turn, follow and pass him. He now drives alongside my car; he flags me; lowers his window; makes desperate gestures for me to drive on and accelerates recklessly. I heard one word: hospital. I will not road-race; who does he think I am?

Sheets of rain are beating down on the pavement, visibility is next to nil; I will have to stop driving if I don't want to end up in a ditch. Just my luck, I have an urgent need to pee. I hope I can find a gas station soon; old bladders are weak. A fellow senior I met on my daily walks told me that he carries a milk bottle in his car just to pee in whenever the need arises. We women are at a disadvantage regarding the passing of water. My cheeks, my thighs, my toes are in tight knots. Funny, when your body calls for attention all other worries or intellectual musing take a hike. There is a school of thought that claims that poor people are more stupid than affluent ones. Well, it is hard to concentrate on the Pythagoras's theorem while your stomach is shrinking for lack of grub.

I can't wait any longer, I stop on the side of the road, cover my head with a plastic shopping bag abandoned on the back seat and squat my back resting on the open car door. Not a second too soon. Relief! Now I can resume mulling over Robin's disclosures.

Robin: Edgar's son; Edgar: Robin's Uncle Ed. No wonder I had a flash of recognition when I first saw him. Edgar, born of an Irish mother and an Italian father who only stayed long enough to give him a much hated name and who could not or would not do that to his own son. Edgar, who cared enough to give some privileged time to his son. Loving, tender, weak Edgar who had never learned how to be a father and settled on being an uncle. Edgar, who shot himself dead in his car the very day he had announced to the ones he cared for that he had finally found the Holy Grail; a way to propel himself of the endless circus of neediness. Was he so ashamed that he never could share his secret with me? Did I turn a blind eye to what was eating him? Was I that callous, thoughtless, engrossed in my own needs that I did not give him the space he needed? Something does not add up. I am missing important clues and I think Robin can help. There are no coincidences. Is this an opportunity to redeem myself? I will protect your Robin, Edgar, I promise.

I have always believed my maternal instinct was nonexistent, very much like my own mother who only developed a protective shield for me after she died. As a child I was in her way, hindering more serious activities like golfing, playing bridge or exercising at the spa. I had sporadic nannies until I was six years old and then I was either at my paternal grandparents or at the neighbour's. My father must have been a busy man too for I only remember him from pictures my grandma showed me. He died when I was eight, I am not even sure I was present at the funeral. Anyway, I have no recollection of it. My grandma was fine, especially after she took a night cap which she started to sip and refill from early morning on. As long as I did not bother her she did not bother me. We had an understanding. Then there was the wonderful, neighbour's big messy house. Mrs. Carey was its engine. She kept running up and down the stairs with loads of laundry, or food or kids. She was very loud. She laughed and screamed all the time and she even found time to play hop-scotch with us. She said it was to see sooner the face of the next little one who was in her belly. I remember wishing it was me. She called me Poor Clara. At the time I did not understand why Poor. I read a lot, cookbooks, bridge magazines, my father's law books.

I did not know at the time that you had to understand what you read. Maybe this is why now I read books on physics when I don't really have a clue. I rely on quantum consciousness, that supposedly universal consciousness our brain is connected to according to the latest and much contested physicists' theory.

Back home?

I did it again; I drifted into the "Then". Sorry. I better keep in my "Now". I have been driving along and approaching town. I am going straight to the hospital to join Cynthia, the botched up aging Romeo and possibly Robin if I understood what he meant. The big rain storm is relenting. There I go, back on track!

I better take a few deep breaths before jumping back into the turmoil. Phew, and to think that two weeks ago I was wishing for some excitement in my boring life. I must have been wishing it very strongly. There are some serious philosophers and even some of the new scientists, the quantum kind, who believe that we actually create our own reality. I wish I would have concentrated more on the frog whispering thing. Now I would be flying to the Amazon, courtesy of National Geographic, to establish a possible relationship between the common frogs of Siberia and the endangered species down there. That would have been more fun. Yet I can't complain too much, this adventure is a trip too. A trip into my grossly unknown self.

Robin is knocking on the car door. He is dripping wet. I unlock the doors, he gets in.

"Please, don't drop me. I need you. You are the first sane person I have met since my mother died." He pleads.

Sane person? Now I know he is deluded.

"Look Robin, I like you a lot, but I am completely broke. I must return home and I don't even know how I can do that. This car is not mine. I did not pay for the rental. The fellow, who rented it for me, wants it returned. I am more stranded than you think. There are also other issues that I have not told you about that make me a dangerous person to know. But when all is sorted out, if it sorts out; here is my phone number, call me when you are in town and we will have a nice chat." I say in a firm tone of voice.

"I have a little bit of money, that could buy you at least another week in the motel, later on I will have some more and you could find a nice place here. I would come and visit you. We could have a grand time. I will get a car for you. I have a good job now."

He sounds just like an eight year old boy. This is Edgar all over again. What is it with these guys, they get themselves in a mess and they come running to Mamma scared of the big bad wolf. Who do they think I am? What do they want from me? I don't even have big boobs to comfort them and I sure don't know anything about the worlds they seem to get into.

"I will think about it, but right now I must go and see my friends. There are a few things I would like to discuss with you. So phone the motel to check if I am still there, if not call me in two or three days at the number I gave you. So long Robin! " I leave to check what is happening on the other front.

Macky is dressed in 'civvies' in a wheel chair. His right arm in a sling, a big patch on his eyes and hooked to an oxygen tank to help with his breathing. I guess his broken ribs make it difficult for him to breathe. His one eye has the glazed look of a druggie. Cynthia is standing by. She has the jitters. She is clasping her hands together and her lower jaw is trembling as if she was having an attack of cerebral palsy.

"You said, you would be back soon and you were gone for two hours!", she says reproachfully.

"I came back as soon as I could. I had to sort out my affairs at the bank." I don't know what sorts of affairs I have with the bank since I am mostly living a buck at a time; but I think that is an excuse they can buy.

"Well, Macky has decided that he wants to go home. I phoned and we can book a flight leaving at six tonight. We would like you to drive us first to the motel, so I can pick up my stuff and then to the airport, MyDear."

Just what I thought, these two only look after themselves and to hell with Clara. Well good riddance! I will have to hitch a ride back home. It's a long ride. Maybe I could take on Robin's offer; I don't know.

It takes a while to settle Macky on the back seat with all his hospital gear. Cynthia had to sign his release, against the doctor's advice, and I had to witness since Macky can't sign. In the motel parking lot, Harvey is busy around his truck, Jeo is with him. As soon as the child sees me, he runs to hug me.

"Granny Clara, I am so glad to see you, I know a big secret that I am not supposed to tell. When are your two friends leaving?" he whispers in my ear.

"Very soon. I am going to take them to the airport. They are flying back home."

"Good, they don't smell nice."

No time to discuss olfactory perceptions with Jeo, Cynthia is calling me from inside the suite and Macky is moaning on the back seat where we left him since it is too much of a hassle to get him out and then in again. Harvey is winking at me and makes desperate little signs to get my attention. I am very much in demand. I will tackle Cynthia first.

She is in the bathroom sobbing.

"What is happening to you MyDear?" I might as well call her that too, "You are the one who is leaving me stranded in Prince Rupert. Is this why you are crying? I seem to remember that you called me your friend but you have more important business with Macky the fool." I hiss.

"Oh Clara, what can I do? The poor man is suffering I cannot leave him all by himself. After all he is in this mess because he wanted to help us."

I shout "No, he is in this mess because he is a stupid jerk; he still thinks he is irresistible with his dyed hair and his lipstick. He is a goner, a wash out, a has-been. He refused to listen to you when you told him that the goon was on board. Now he put you and possibly me in more danger; I have no sympathy for him. He is your friend not mine. Do what you want and don't come running to me for support. So, goodbye and good luck!" I slam the bathroom door and hope everyone heard me.

My anger is shooting waves down my extremities. I would not be surprised if the walls of the suite would explode or implode whatever. I give a good kick to the coffee table and I hurt my big toe. I know my eyes are shooting darts full of venom. And…

I fall on the sofa laughing hysterically cltching my toe. That's it, each time I reach a real good peak of anger and I am ready to punch somebody for relief, I start laughing. My ballooned ego deflates in an instant. It is not fair. Now I am going to feel sorry for the miserable blind clown whose sex-appeal is dwindling away mercilessly. I laugh and I cry all at once. The aging process can be so cruel to some people. I cry over myself and over all the poor geysers that for a fair part of their lives relied on their good looks, or their wealth, or their strength and feel it streaming away from them irretrievably. One feels so empty, so lost, so humiliated.

Macky is not such a bad egg; he is paying a steep price for a last dance. Although there is a tendency lately to accept homosexuality, considering Macky's age he must have suffered a lot of discrimination in school and elsewhere even if his family supported him, which is not likely. The man, as I met him, has retained a caring attitude, a love of fun. And I am a bully; I have got to apologize to Cynthia.

She is sitting on the floor, her back resting on the side of the bathtub, her hair looks a mess, she is very pale, and her lips are trembling uncontrollably. I sit beside her; I hug her and give her a big kiss.

"I am sorry; I was completely out of line. Of course I understand that it is your duty to accompany Macky, Old Girl. I am with you."

"Oh Clara, I will miss you terribly. It has been a very long time since somebody kissed me like you did just now. Thank you." She rests her head on my shoulder and I feel a rush of true affection towards her.

"It is a long time for me too that I felt so close to someone." If she asked me right now I would be willing to seal our friendship with a drop of blood from the tip of my finger. Will I ever grow up!

She stands up, brushes her pants, looks in the mirror, has a little yelp, repaints her lips and fixes her hair. She is all business again.

I help her pack her things; she looks at me and says "You know what; we are about the same size you and I, why don't I leave some of my clothes with you. Some of it I never wore, if you don't like them you could always give them to the Salvation Army. It will be much easier if I have fewer bags to look after at the airport with Macky incapacitated as he is, Poor Soul. And by the way how are you faring money wise?"

This is a very touchy subject for me. I never discuss my money with anybody. I get by and that's it. I will never be seen at a food bank or at any of the free meals served at churches. My budget is my own business. I will not borrow money that I can't give back. So, I say "I'll manage." Light-heartedly. I am not going to tell her that I plan to hitchhike my way back. She would be horrified and maybe she would pity me. That I could not take. This is one of my big hang-ups, a stupid pride. I am not wanting! I am not needy! I get by; fuck off. I am shutting off; I am not letting people in. What am I scared of? Losing my independence? Having to say thank you? Being indebted by something a lot pricier than money or material goods? I am acting no better than a church bigot while I pride myself to be liberal minded, a free spirit. What a hoax!

This "Now" thing is not amusing anymore; it forces me into corners of myself that I don't care to explore. Leave it to my imaginative biographers. The land of "Then" is way more magical as Stephen King noted in one of his last books. You can twist it, adorn it, sift it and even believe it. This is why we old cronies relish lulling in it.

While I have been mulling over my shortcomings Cynthia finished her preparation for departure. She is writing a cheque.

"Look Clara, I think it is dangerous for the three of us to be seen together. So you would do us a favour if you drove back home with the rented car. If I remember well we can return the car to any one of the company offices. Will you do that for us? I am leaving some money I hope it will be enough to cover extended rental and gas for the trip with a little extra for incidentals."

For one thing that is the third time she calls me Clara and not MyDear. That counts for something. Then she is tactful, she acknowledges my fucking pride. To think that I took her for a fool! I should tell her what information I got from Robin. There is no time left though if they are to catch that flight. We should go. I say:"OK" and I pick up the cheque. It is for eight hundred dollars. I don't thank her, maybe next time.

We wave goodbye to Harvey and Jeo, I don't forget to tell them that I will be back soon. Macky is not well, I am starting to worry about his decision to fly back so early after the attack. Cynthia sits in front since the oxygen tank takes a lot of room in the back. The flight takes three hours and there will be at least another hour before they are home. I try to convince them to go directly to a hospital but Macky is adamant. He wants to be home. He says that he has a doctor friend he trusts who will be able to come to his place. I don't think he is well enough to be contradicted.

At the airport, another big problem, they don't want to board Macky with the oxygen tank. They say it is standard regulations.

They will supply him with their own oxygen and will phone to have another rented tank at arrival. For the airline to supply the oxygen in flight will cost an extra six hundreds dollars. All told that little escapade will have cost both of them an arm and a leg, and possibly an eye too without counting the broken ribs. The three of us are in a real funky mood. I wave goodbye again. It is becoming a habit now.

I go to the bank to deposit Cynthia's cheque because it will take a good three days to clear. The rental car is due back in two days. Even if I am sure Cynthia's money is good, I might still have to hitchhike my way back because I am broke again. I dare not spend my regular income on extras since my budget is so tight. That reminds me that my rent is past due, knowing Marge, the superintendant's wife, she will be in a stew. I hope she does not decide to evict me which is something the owner would love to do. I have been at that place for a few years and my rent is ridiculously low compared to the newer tenants. By law the owners can only increase the rent by a small percentage per year but when they get new tenants they can always claim that they renovated and thus justify much higher rates. I will phone Marge as soon as I reach the motel. All my other bills I pay online. So I just have to go to the library tomorrow and tend to my affairs.

Home base

There is one car parked at Harvey's Paradise. Good for Harvey, one more customer. He needs it. I have hardly kicked my shoes off that Jeo is knocking at the door. He lets himself in since I had not locked the door.

"Do you know what? There are two letters for you at the desk but Daddy did not want me to bring them to you. He wants to give them to you himself. I think he likes you."

"Is that the secret you were not supposed to tell?"

"No, I am going to have another brother or sister. I am not telling anyone."

"Is this good news for you?" I ask while massaging my feet.

"I don't know, my other friend has lots of little brothers and sisters. He says that they are a pain in the neck. Especially babies because they cry and poo and pee all the time and can't talk. His mommy says she does not have time to talk; his Dad does not come home anymore. My friend puts glue in a paper bag and sniffs it. He says it makes him feel better. When he does that, his eyes look funny and he does not talk anymore. So I am not sure and Daddy is not sure either. I heard him talk about 'a bortion' that would solve the problem. Mommy is crying. Please come to my house. Grandpa is gone for a big celebration and I am scared of the '*bortion*'." He gives me a hug.

I put my shoes back on pick up the car keys and get ready to go.

"I think we deserve a treat. Do you want to come with me? Ask your mum, we will be gone for twenty minutes."

"Where are we going?"

"I can't tell; it's a surprise." I thought I had problems. It's a breeze compared to this little boy's. Within seconds Jeo is back in my car with his special booster seat.

"Did you ever sniff glue?" I ask in a noncommittal tone of voice.

"Yes, Bruce let me try it once. It made me very sick. The principal called my Dad. My dad said that if I did it again he would give me the strap. Grandpa cried and said it was a curse. Mommy was crying too and banged pots in the kitchen. She always does that when she is unhappy."

We are now choosing donuts, Jeo has forgotten all his troubles. He asks how many we are allowed. When I say a dozen he asks me if it's equal to twelve. I remark that he is super good in math and he says that is not what his teacher thinks. He chooses the double chocolate sprinkled with colourful candies. He has some concern about how many of us are going to share the twelve and particularly how many I am going to eat. We have a lengthy discussion on the pros and cons of sharing and we are back at the motel with a box full of sugary junk food.

Jeo is certainly not disappointed to have put his trust in me. I get five stars as far as he is concerned. As for me, I give myself four and a half. I hate to brag. '*Bortions*' or not we are beaming. June, Jeo's mum makes herb tea that tastes delicious. And we all share the donuts happily. June says that she will come by later to my suite to see if everything is OK. I understand that she needs to talk. Harvey says that he has received some mail for me and would I pass by the office or should he bring it to my room later. I tell him that there is no rush and I could pick it up later and I leave as they are ready to put the children to bed. I feel pretty tired myself but I don't think the day is over yet. As I step out, I breathe the lovely air of late summer, almost fall and although this has been a very busy and troubling day I don't feel bad at all. As a matter of fact I am in a good mood. I put two chairs out, one to sit on, the other for my feet. I relax in a blissful moment of solitude. The storm earlier cleared the air. My contemplation is not going to last very long. June is approaching dragging a plastic patio chair close to mine. She smiles, I smile. She is a lovely young woman and she obviously knows how to keep quiet. After a good fifteen minutes of each of us in our own thoughts I better break the spell. I guess she is near me for a reason.

"Children are sleeping?"

"Yes. Jeo is very excited about meeting you. That's all he talks about. It is nice to have you around."

"I am happy I met your family, I hope when I am gone that we can keep in touch. Do you know how to use a computer? Send email? Use Skype?"

"A little, but Jeo is learning and he will teach me. Harvey is too impatient with me. I am not a good writer. Do you have children of your own?"

"I wish I had, but it did not work for me. I don't think I could have been as good a mother as you are."

Tears are rolling down her cheeks.

"What is wrong June? Can I help?"

"I am pregnant. Harvey and I don't want another child. It is hard enough with two and now that the little one will soon go to school, I wanted to go back to school too and finish my high school. I dropped out in grade nine. Make something out of myself. So Jeo later on would not be ashamed of me."

"How far along are you?"

"Two months. Harvey wants me to have an abortion."

"What about you? What do you want?"

I don't know; if I do the people in church are not going to talk to me anymore. They say it is a horrible sin."

"Do you believe that?"

"I don't know. Harvey does not go to church and his father, Grandpa, does not either. They say we have to return to our own beliefs. They say that the churches have done enough damage to us. But I like the singing and it is fun to have friends. I feel so lonely sometimes."

"Tell you what. Tomorrow I have to go to the library. I can look up some information for you. The more you know the better it will be to make a choice. You are the one to decide."

"Why don't you tell me what to do?"

"Look June, you are a beautiful, intelligent young woman, I don't think anybody should tell you what to do. Whatever you decide will be perfect I am sure; as long as you don't have to say so and so made me do it." I give her a big hug and a kiss. I have become a kisser lately. She holds me tight.

Harvey is approaching. June gets up and leaves. The tension is palpable between these two. I am sure they think they put up a good show in front of the children. Jeo is not a fool and I will keep his secret.

"Two different men showed up at the motel today asking for you. One you know for sure because he was with you yesterday. He paid for your room for another week. I think his name is Robin. The other asked if a woman called Clara was still at the motel and he left this for you. Is Robin any kind of relation? He likes you a lot. The other one was nice and polite but he gave me the creeps."

Oh, oh! For a moment I had almost forgotten the mess I am in. The runaway witness business is not a plum job. I shove the heavy envelope Harvey hands me deep in my pocket. I will tend to it later when I am alone. Harvey sits on the hot chair June occupied a moment ago. The night is settling in. The forest in the background has turned very quiet. Even the crows are taking a break from their constant arguing. There is an occasional whoosh of a car passing by on the road. Only the crickets keep busy. I thank Harvey. Harvey obviously is a man of few words yet sitting by me I sense that he has more to say. I hope I can help.

"Do you have children of your own? You must, because children are very much taken by you. Jeo for one; he is ready to adopt you as his official Granny. Grandparents are very important with our people. They are the ones that pass on the knowledge." He pauses as if he is scared to speak further. I wait, there is more to come and I am resolute to lend him my ears.

"My father is doing his best but he was not always like that. He used to be a lousy drunk. He left my mother with five of us to look after. My mother herself was hitting the sauce. It was hell. The day she passed on, I swore I would never touch the stuff. June had a similar experience with her parents. Twelve years ago, a cousin, a fisherman with his own boat took my father on board. The boat was dry. Not a drop of alcohol could be found. My father had a huge withdrawal crisis in the middle of the ocean. Then as dawn broke he heard the Raven. The Raven gave him back his pride. He says the sun was sparkling myriads of stars on the ocean waves. He said for the first time in his life he felt like being an important part of the universe. He has not drunk since. He went back to the reserve, relearned our language, the rituals of our clan and has become like a missionary for our people. I am proud of him."

"That's a beautiful story you are telling me, Harvey. Thank you for sharing it. I would love to participate sometime in a ritual if I could be allowed, being an outsider."

"I am convinced that when my father sees you he will recognize you as one of us. Belonging is not a matter of blood line. It is a matter of common awareness, consciousness I should say. I think you have it even though you might not realize it." He closes his eyes, and abruptly he blurts:"As a woman how do you feel about abortion?" After all these roundabout ways we are finally where he intended to be. The crux of his worry.

"I am neither for nor against. Giving birth is a very scary affair for a woman. Not the actual delivery process but the twenty years of mothering commitment it implies. If a woman does not want this commitment, both the child to be and the mother are better off to abort. To me it is entirely the woman's choice. The pregnant young woman needs information devoid of so-called 'moral' precepts which are all hogwash as far as I am concerned. I must admit though that in my books, abortion is a last resort. In our country nowadays young people who do not want to have children have a few more clever options available to them."

It is interesting how we all want to be victims of circumstances, we want to delegate responsibility for what we consider our ills to higher authorities, be it God, Fate, parents or whatever and whomever we fancy. I will not walk into that. I bid goodnight to Harvey and go to my suite. I have thinking to do on my own. I make myself a cup of Cynthia's tea and go to bed. I leave the thinking part for tomorrow.

I must have been exhausted, it's three AM, my cup of tea is three quarters full, I am still in my street clothes and I am staring at the ceiling. I go to the bathroom without turning the lights on; I sit in a daze wondering where these past four or five hours went. I undress, finish my cold cup of tea return to bed and lie there trying to relive yesterday's happenings. Robin, Cynthia, Macky, Jeo, June, Harvey…

I get up and dig out the envelope Harvey handed to me. It contains a letter with a lawyer's letterhead and another sealed envelope.

Dear Mrs Vittorio,

On behalf of my client who prefers to remain anonymous I offer my sincere regret for the misunderstanding about the use of the cabin you seemed to believe was at your disposal since the unfortunate event of your husband's death.

My client wishes you to acknowledge that the arrangement passed between your husband and himself concerning the property was only temporary and in no way binding or even less transferable to next of kin.

My client anticipates your disappointment in the matter and wishes to compensate you with what he deems a fair conclusion.

This is a onetime deal as long as you accept that you no longer have any reason to sojourn in his rightful property. No answer is necessary. Your acceptance of the gift will be proof of your agreement in this matter and any further presence of yours on the site would be considered as trespassing.

My client also wishes me to add that after meeting with you he regards you as a very honourable lady and is certain that you will understand the need not to archive this message in any way.

Yours truly and best of luck.

The sealed envelope contains fifteen one hundred dollar bills. Now I am totally awake. I can't believe my luck! I reread the letter and reread it again. The envelope has no postmark, it was hand delivered. I make myself another cup of tea and I finish up all the cookies and the carrots and the whipped cream. I sit on the side of the bed and contemplate tearing the letter to pieces. No I think I will buy a lighter and burn it on the side of a road or in a park fire pit. I am rolling in dough! La, la, la. I am going for a huge breakfast with six slices of bacon later on and then I'll buy a new pair of shoes to replace the one I lost in the restaurant and a real leather strap for my watch and treat myself to a salon haircut. And get some wild smoked salmon. And, and, and, I am so excited I am pacing up and down my room in a frenzy. As if I cared about the blasted cottage. I never liked that placed. I would not have gone back anyway. This is the best deal I ever had in my life. "Honourable lady' indeed I feel like a swindler. It feels good. A nice tickle inside. Like the day I went to the Casino with Edgar I was playing at a nickel machine when all of a sudden the machine started to puke coins and coins. At first I thought I had inadvertently broken the machine. I won four buckets full of coins. Four hundred dollars! Now machines don't puke money anymore they issue vouchers that you can redeem at other machines. It is not as much fun; you don't hear the money clinking down. My casino days were sparse then and are nonexistent now. I only went with Edgar. As a grand lord, he would give me two, sometime three twenty dollar bills, wish me luck and go and play poker. This was when he was flush with money. If he had had a 'good day', as he called it, we would treat ourselves with a scrumptious dinner and head back home singing along with the radio blaring full blast. I miss you Edgar. I feel like dancing with you, you miserable liar.

Shape up, Clara; you are again drifting in the Then!

I better start thinking about my next move. Let's move to the 'Later'. I lie in bed, staring at the ceiling where different possible scenarios unfold. Should I drive back via the long road, fly, take the ferry? Should I go home or stay here another week as Robin obviously wants me to do? Nothing or nobody awaits me back home. Well, Cynthia maybe, probably…She paid for the return trip… On the other hand I have the excuse to stay a few more days waiting for her cheque to be honoured at the bank therefore catering to my procrastination and the enticing thought that Inaction is Action. Cool, cool!...

The team

All this rumination must have put me to sleep. It is nine o'clock on my watch and there is a knock at the door. I hope it is not Jeo with another secret. I have had my fill of secrets for the next ten years. I long to return to my computer where all secrets can be elucidated through Wikipedia.

I quickly put the money and the letter under the pillow.

It's Robin holding two cups of coffee and a bag of goodies in a cardboard tray. He stands at the door. What is wrong with him? Why doesn't he chase girls his age?

"Did you have breakfast yet?" he says with a shy smile. It's such an eerie feeling to see him like that. I am bewitched. I try to act grumpy without success. "I have a lot to tell you. Hope you are ready for some shaky news." He adds stepping into the suite.

More shaky news! This confirms the information you get from the book the 'Law of Attraction', like attracts like. Since I met the cat bad news, shaky news is pouring. That handsome cat cast a spell on me. No kidding.

"Let me have my coffee first." I beg in a whining tone. I plop on a chair and I sip ever so slowly the dark sweet juice. Robin is fretting, impatient, jittery.

"I don't have much time. I don't want anybody to spot my car in the motel. This morning the police found one of the dead guys in the park. I know because I heard it on the police radio band. But there is more. You remember Tony, the man who hired me? Well I am almost sure that he is the one who put the contract on the men. I heard him talk on the phone before he left. He was saying that two of the psychos have been taken care of."

"Robin can you show me on the map the cabin you are working from?" I ask and I hope against hope that it's not where I think it is. That his Tony is not my Tony. *"Should I tell him what I know? Would that help him? Would it help me? Can I trust Robin? Isn't he baiting me?"* I keep drinking my coffee and nibbling on the muffin trying to assess the situation, My situation. Only the goon walking in the restaurant saw me. Is he one of the dead guys or is he the one on the cruise ship who mauled poor Macky and was looking for Cynthia? Right now I better let Robin talk since he is in a talkative mood. I risk losing his trust in me if he finds out I am more aware of the going-ons of this whole affair than he probably thinks.

I feel boxed in a messy business having no idea how it is going to end. All the contemporary know-it-all gurus tell you that we are not boxed in, that through an exercise of mind over matter you can do quantum leaps to wherever you want to be. But isn't it jumping from one box into another box? For my part I rather like to explore my boxes because I believe that there are always one or more jewels in it if I search well. In this particular box I've already discovered Cynthia, Robin not forgetting the pure little gem Jeo. I am not counting what I learned about myself in such a short time. The big rush of tenderness for others that I thought I had completely exhausted on Edgar. That feeling of belonging outside my comfort zone of isolation. I am not the outsider I proudly believed I was. I am part of that silly world.

Robin is looking at me very concerned. I was lost in my thoughts and I forgot about him.

"Excuse me Robin, I started thinking of something but I am back with you now." I apologize.

"Do you know anything about the Union? BC Bud? The cannabis industry?"

"No, not much, just that I don't think that marijuana should be illegal."

"I learned a lot in jail. Like the Calgary born Tommy Chong said when he got out of his nine month stint in a US jail. Jail changes you. I could talk to you for hours on the subject."

"Robin, you did not come here to lecture me. Get on with it, stop beating around the bush."

"Yeah, I know. It's that I don't want to scare you and I want to scare you.

When I first met Tony, I was very impressed. He looked to me like a cool guy who knew what he was doing. He told me he wanted to produce the best stuff on the market. He was interested in hash because it is supposed to be better than smoking marijuana. He wanted to make it with plants that had not been exposed to pesticide. He spent all kinds of time with me to explain his goal. But now that I saw the two fellows leave the cabin and a few hours later I saw the same two in the park where they shot the men I told you about. I think that Tony is a ruthless man who takes the law into his own hands. Maybe you will think that I am naïve, that I should have foreseen this. I did not. It is a lot more than I bargained for. I admit that if what I read in the paper is true, these guys were psychos who shot innocent patrons along with whomever they were paid to punish. No, I don't want to be part of this. The way I understood my job was to receive the bud, make the best bubble hash out of it and somebody would pick it up for distribution. Yes, I was given a gun, but that was to be used strictly in case I was robbed. The cabin is very isolated and I would have a lot of cash at hand to pay the grow-op people delivering the raw material."

Robin is very pale he is restless on the chair, he keeps wiping his forehead, rubs his hands on his thighs, his heels are dancing a little jig of their own, he is very scared. I get up to make coffee. I wish I had something to lace it with. That used to calm Edgar when he was distraught. I am not to feed his fear. I have to let it run its course.

"So, Robin, why don't you call it quits?" I say handing him his second cup of coffee.

"I can't, that's what I am trying to explain to you. I owe Tony a lot of money. I had maxed out my credit. I had been kicked out of my apartment, no wheels. No jobs and no prospect of one. Tony gave me enough money to pay my debts, he let me use one of his cars, gave me a job. I owe him bundles. I am stuck!"

"You paid my motel fees with some of Tony's money?"

"Kind of." he blurts shyly.

"Where else have you spent money foolishly, Robin?" I can't believe it; this is a boy in a man's body!

"I just paid the bank and bought some hiking outfits. That's all. It is not foolish to try to have you stay close by. I like you."

"Robin, you don't know the first thing about me. "

"I know you like nature; I know you can be funny. I think you are the first sane person I have met in a long time. You remind me of my mother that I miss so much. Please be my friend!"

Damned Robin, he did it again. I can't resist him. My self-defence mechanism is destroyed. I must be craving affection. This little niche of supposed independence, non-commitment I have carved for myself is very fragile indeed and about to be exposed as a crock; blown in my face. The hypothetical son of mine needs help; I want to help, I need to help; will I know what to say? I keep sipping my coffee silently to gain time to find the right words. I am not ready to tell him the reason I am in this part of the country, or about Uncle Ed, even less about Tony's letter or money. None of this will do him any good; it would just unduly burden him and let's admit it put me at risk.

I should be honest with myself, I am still not sure I can trust him.

I wish I had some motherly experience.

His apparent need to befriend me is puzzling.

It feels good to be wanted but I don't want to be too naive.

I have been duped by charming guys before.

It is interesting how this seemingly wise pondering is nothing but a reflection of my cowardice confronted by the yearning of my heart to give in, to love freely, to open up to joy. Shy, calculating dried up soul that I am. What is wrong with me, why can't I let go of my fears? I can and I will. To hell with Mind over Matter, reason, and all that shit! Life is short especially for me. I will follow my heart.

"You know, Robin, the instant I saw you in the park I felt drawn to you. As strange as it may seem from an old woman like me, I feel we are kin, your remind me of someone to whom I gave my heart once. So of course I want to be your friend."

And I tell it all. Edgar alias Uncle Ed, the cabin, the cat, the restaurant massacre, Macky and his broken ribs, Tony. Everything. Robin is fascinated; he paces the room, stops once in a while for clarification, hits his left fist in his opened right hand, slaps his face, sits on the bed and jumps up again. Balances on a chair and falls off it backward, bounces back up without noticing it. *I wish I could do that.* Combs his fingers through his hair at length. Opens the fridge and finishes the whipping cream and the carrots.

"Auntie Clara, where is the cat? I want to meet him. I dreamed of it."

"Robin, my boy, let's make a team. Together we can sort things out. We must remain level-headed to assess our situation."

There is a knock at the door, Robin opens it; it's Jeo with a note in his hand. He says that a man called and he wants Robin to call him back as soon as possible, he wants Granny Clara to call him too at that number.

"You are not in school today, Jeo?" I ask.

"No, I have the mumps" he grins. "If you want to get it too just kiss me on the lips and I'll give it to you. It's real cool. See my ears? Daddy calls me Dumbo. I hope it lasts a whole year. I am not going to let my sister, Turnip, kiss me though because she is a pest." And with that he winks devilishly and skips his way out.

Who said that at my age it was too late to start a family? In a little over a fortnight I have found a sister, Cynthia, a mangled half brother, Macky, a son, Robin and even a grandson, Jeo. I am glad to confirm that spiritual genes weigh more than physical ones.

"How did Tony know you were with me, here in this motel?"

"I have not the slightest idea. My cell is turned off. I did not tell anyone where I was going. Anyway I am alone in the cabin now. Tony left yesterday."

"This Tony must be a very clever and powerful man to have survived in this business for so long. He must also have a huge network of business acquaintants all over North America. For these reasons I have a lot of respect for him; not because he is rich and powerful but because he knows what he wants and goes and gets it. There are so many meek people who never stop blaming fate for their cold feet. Robin, my son, this is not a coincidence that you found him in your path. There is a lesson for you and for myself, I must admit, in Tony's accomplishment. I am not saying that what you want is what he wants; but study how he goes about it. Many people get into this business and get burnt as we have witnessed, don't be one of them." I moralize with a stern kindergarten teacher's conviction. "I wonder why this Tony wants to talk to me too."

So far, I feel ahead of the game, without even trying I have been paid over two thousand bucks to stay away from a cabin I detest that would have given me rheumatoid arthritis not to mention constipation.

If Robin's information is correct, and I believe him, the third goon is not going to last very long. I am safe and Cynthia and Macky are too. If Tony is the kind of person I think he is Robin is not in immediate danger as long as he plays fair and square with him. We must remain alert though for any developments.

"Do you know of any harm done by using Bubble hash?" I ask Robin.

"No, none whatsoever, on the contrary. A lot of artists, creative people use it regularly. It is better than pot; especially if it is produced with the best plants."

"Do you have any intentions to bypass Tony while being employed by him?"

"Absolutely none."

"Then I think Robin that you are relatively safe for now and so am I. Now you better return his call. I will call him a bit later when you are gone. Let's stay in touch. I will be at the motel another two or three days, then I will go back home by ferry. You have my home phone and here is my address. I am very happy to have found you and that we are friends. I am on my way to the library to check my email and look up some information for June, Harvey's wife."

Robin leaves not before hugging my five foot three, one hundred pound body so tight against his six foot three frame, my nose pressing on his ribs that I wonder why my lungs did not collapse all together.

"I feel strong now Auntie, with you on my side I will lick this thing and even come out ahead. You are going to be my lighthouse" he says and yes he looks taller and full of confidence. I have no idea what I did to him and it does not matter but I know I heard someone else tell me that with just exactly the same word. It makes me shiver.

"No, no Clara, stay in the Now. Let go of the Then! You have been given another chance. Don't mess it up."

On my way to the library, I rehash what Robin told me. I stop at Tony's phone messages. It was relatively easy for him to find me. There are not that many motels on the road from the cabin to Prince Rupert. Judging from my financial means I would have chosen cheap over fancy. So a few phone calls and bingo, he located me. What about Robin? How did Tony know he was visiting me? Did Robin talk to him about me? What about Harvey? The day I checked in he subtly let me know that he stocked weed. Has he got a connection with Tony? Is he a snitch? Could be. Why did he invite us for supper? Friendly conviviality or trying to find out more about us? Maybe both. Could the motel be a front for other shady activities? I wonder and I am going to be extra careful.

I got a computer at the library and I do some research to evaluate the best way for me to return home. Rail, ferry, air, or drive. The ferry is my first choice. There is one every Friday. It is a day of sailing, twenty hours letting me off at Port Hardy at the northern tip of Vancouver Island, then three hundred kilometre ride to Nanaimo where I would board another ferry to Vancouver. If I take a cabin it would cost me a bare minimum of six hundred dollars but it is a lovely trip along the inside passage between the mainland and Vancouver Island with stopovers at Klemtu and Bella Bella. There is no train going directly to Vancouver. Every other day a passenger train leaves for Jasper, Alberta in the middle of the Rockies. It stops over night in Prince George where you must reserve a hotel room. It is a two day trip to Jasper, and then you must stay one night in Jasper to catch the next train to Vancouver, another twenty hour ride. A beautiful four day trip through the most gorgeous scenery for the mere sum of eight hundred dollars. I am not in the mood to drive back the way I came. That leaves the plane. There are two two-hour flights daily for three hundred dollars. I think my choice is clear even though I am richer than I have been in the past fifteen years I don't want to squander my money foolishly when I don't know what to expect when I get back home. I cannot make my reservation online since I don't have a credit card. I will go to a travel agency with my cash. I will try to catch a flight the day after tomorrow. That will leave time to pack all the stuff Cynthia left with me; return the car at the airport and perhaps go for another stroll in a park. I want to avoid the one where I met Robin for the first time because it must be teaming with cops.

Next I look up some information for June. Apparently there is a serious problem of venereal disease and teenage pregnancies in the back country. Since most people live in small communities; teenagers shy away from getting the right protection and buying condoms for fear it would be reported to their parents. Fortunately for June there is a service in town that could help her in making the right choice about her condition. I could invite her for a coffee downtown if she is not too busy with the kids and the mumps and show her what I found. We could turn it into a nice outing; it might be interesting to go and visit the museum of Tsimshian artefacts with her. It would add another dimension to the exhibit and maybe get her mind off her worries.

For some reason, I cannot yet define, I do not feel at ease to return Tony's call from the motel. I will call him from a public phone booth. With the cell phone mania nowadays it is more and more difficult to find a phone booth in operating condition; I should not have given Macky's cell back. So I return to the library and ask to use their line. It does not work because it is an out of town number. The librarian tells me to go to the airport or to the railway station. She is sure that I can find a public phone that works at either of these places. She used one there less than a week ago. I will drive to the airport and maybe I can check into reservations for a flight the day after tomorrow.

The suave and debonair Tony is true to himself. He calls me darling Clara, inquires about my health and my sojourn in Prince Rupert. Tells me how impressed he had been by me. Assures me that he thinks highly of my intelligence, my presence of mind, my 'unbelievable fitness for an old girl like me'. In other words his opinion of me is way up. What he really was wondering is if I should not mind rendering him a 'little service'. Since he is sure I will fly back to Vancouver very soon now, would I mind to include in my luggage a small parcel he forgot while up here. Someone would deliver it to me at the motel, it would be all wrapped up and not take much space. Of course he would assume the cost of the trip; another someone would wait for me on arrival in town to pick the said package up. He adds that he often has a need for a really 'trustworthy' person to make errands of the same nature. Should I be interested he would make it fairly rewarding for the right person.

He himself is very flighty and keeps forgetting important things when he travels.

Does this Tony think I am a dumb broad or what? Isn't it what I tried to convey to him back at the motel? Let's keep the game going while I think about joining the Union. 'The Union' as Robin told me is what the whole organization of the industry of BC Buds (the British Columbia Cannabis industry) is commonly called. So I talk a mile a minute about my hemorrhoids that shrank to reasonable proportions, my bunion is not bothering me anymore, the Tim Horton donuts are a whole lot tastier than in Vancouver, they must be frying them in salmon oil; all the while my mind is racing to figure out if I should or should not accept the lucrative and dangerous deal that shark is offering me.

When I am just about to give myself a pat on the back for my cunning, Tony-from-hell cuts me off. "Clara, I get the picture, are you in or not?"

It takes me a second to regain composure. "Yeah!" I say in what I take for a thuggish tone of voice.

"Good, don't play that game anymore with me, it is entertaining but I don't have the time now. Save it for your idiotic friends. Take it easy on the hemorrhoids and lean a bit more on hairdos and nail polish; you will get better results."

"You started the game." I pout.

"I like you Clara; if you were twenty years younger I would marry you." he laughs.

"And you, you are a scumbag I would not touch with a ten foot pole."

"We are going to have fun together. Take the morning flight the day after tomorrow. Pick up your reservation at the counter one hour before departure. Have a nice trip. Bye." He hangs up still giggling.

Another three hundred dollars! If it keeps going like this I will have enough money to pay for my own funeral; in a year or so I might even be able to afford a small mausoleum. Not that I want any of those things, I'd rather be incinerated and my ashes spread at the root of a nice tree on the side where the dogs don't pee. I could also get a face lift, my boobs padded, throw in some false nails and drink a margarita at the Copa Cabana. The possibilities are limitless! Meanwhile I better restock on whipped cream and baby carrots. Robin and Jeo cost me a bundle in that respect.

I am now part of Robin's team. I will meet a lot of people, half of them goons. I dream of flying low over Washington State and dropping bundles of prohibited stuff down the hatch. A new version of Bonnie and Clyde. I have always been a romantic at heart. It is high time for me to live a life of 'depravation'. When I think that only three weeks ago I was bored to death! Now I am super excited. That beats carpet bowling by a long shot. My law-abiding life, my righteousness is nothing but a put-on hiding a fear of law and societal reprisals. I lived for twenty five years with a guy who was an avid gamer. Not only was I blind to his addiction but I never questioned my straight life of the dutiful tow-the-line tax-payer. I erred searching for spiritual enlightenment, half-assedly believing that other people, the ones who made the rules were more advanced than me on the road to wisdom. People like my drinking, nail-polished, golf-playing mother and grandmother, like my lecher-ous lawyer of a father acquainted with many of the rule makers. It must have suited me fine not to get involved. Edgar's death shook me out of my slumber. Not devoting my life to love and to be loved allowed me more time to look around with a critical eye.

The accident

On the way back to the motel I stop at a department store to buy a few toys for the kids, some miniature cars for Jeo and a soft cuddly stuffy for the little girl. She is so cute with her big brown eyes. I also buy an electric slow-cooker for June and Harvey. I get a big bunch of frozen raviolis, some cheese, and a large pail of ice cream. It feels wonderful to be able to treat someone. I really like having the means to splash carelessly. It seems like for ages I haven't been able to do so. From now on I will try to reorganize my budget to do just that. For me it has not only been the excuse of my financial means it is mostly as if I am cracking out of that hard shell that I had built around myself probably for fear of being hurt again. I am alive, I am well. I am on top of the world. This 'Now' stuff is really working. I better buy some wrapping paper to make the pleasure last a few seconds longer.

June does not know about raviolis, so I explain and cook. Everybody likes the dish, and of course the ice cream. I don't think they are being polite because they take second helpings of everything. I tell June that I got information for her. If she wants I can go with her to the clinic or I can babysit and she goes with Harvey. Whatever. For a girl who had her first child when she was not yet seventeen she is doing a marvellous job as a parent. Since it is a lovely evening after the meal we all sit outside. Jeo is playing with his cars in the parking lot. The little girl on her father's lap is cuddling her stuffed teddy bear. It is a lovely family evening where we shoot the breeze about everything and nothing. I sense the fragility and beauty of the moment.

"Why don't you stay with us here, Granny Clara? We need you so much. You belong here." Harvey asks.

"Oh, Yes, Pleaaaaaaase! We could eat 'ravilis' everyday if you want. And when you babysit us we are not going to do any belly-aching; promise." Jeo begs and the little girl smiles.

"We could keep you in the same suite you are in now. This is not a busy place at the best of times. We would make it worth your while." June adds.

I am touched to tears. I love these kids, the four of them.

"Thank you for offering, I am so very fond of the four of you and I am grateful for all the kindness you have shown me. But you don't know really, I am a cranky old woman and you would soon be fed up with me. Besides I don't own a car and here I definitely would need one to get around. Public transit is scarce and unreliable around here..."

There is a loud noise all of a sudden, as if cars are racing on the highway, then the blaring of a police car, no, several police cars sirens blaring through the surrounding trees. A long screech of tires on the pavement, a car makes a u-turn in the parking lot of the motel and runs over Jeo who was squatting playing with his toys. I hear my scream blend with June's echoing in the forest. June faints in my arms; Harvey drops the little girl, rushes to Jeo. The car never stops, nor do the police cars in pursuit. June straggles out of my grip and runs to the boy, the little girl is howling; I pick her up. My heart is beating so hard in my chest I wonder if it is going to burst. "Don't move him!" I yell and I run inside to call 9-1-1 still holding the child.

They say that all their ambulances are out; it might take a good hour before they can make it to the motel. I scream, I beg, I swear.

All useless. I put the little girl down; I run to my room and get a bed sheet, then I take the leaf of the table out. I run back to Jeo, the little girl in tow. Harvey and I carefully wrap Jeo in the sheet while June is holding his hand. Jeo's nose is bleeding. He seems to be in a coma. We slide him on the table leaf and while June and I lift the board Harvey secures the boy with his belt, I hand out my long scarf for a second securing tie. We slide the boy in the back of my car, Harvey drives and I follow in Harvey's truck with the child. Harvey is beside himself; he honks desperately all the way to the hospital. I have a hard time to keep abreast. At the emergency, someone tries to stop me, but I push him aside and scream "Code blue, code blue". A nurse comes out while June and Harvey carry the boy still on the makeshift stretcher. I must calm down, my legs feel like cotton but I don't want to faint. So I hang on to the counter until a doctor is summoned. They think it is all about me. That I have lost my mind. Finally they understand and rush Jeo to the ward while pushing us out of the way. We sit holding hands in the waiting room. An aide comes and hands me a glass of water with a pill of some kind. I drink the water but refuse the medicine. Harvey is sobbing uncontrollably. June stands up; holds her stomach and cries out. A nurse comes and is ready to throw us out. I take a couple of deep breaths and explain that we are in shock and that June is pregnant. They roll out a gurney and take her away. On the loudspeaker someone calls Harvey to the desk. The little girl is wimping, terrified; I take her on my lap and hold her tight whispering a little song in her ear.

It is past midnight now and we haven't heard of Jeo or June. We are sitting desolate amidst a few swearing drunks and undoubtedly beaten women in various states of inebriation. The little girl whose name I now remember, Morgan, is finally asleep curled up on a chair her head resting on my lap. A young doctor approaches us, he says that June has been admitted to the obstetrics ward and that they are waiting for some results for Jeo. No, he has not regained consciousness but has been stabilized, whatever that means. The broken leg is not the problem. The concern is the head injury. They might have to fly him to Vancouver for treatment. They will call us if there are any new developments. The police have been advised and they should come and see us in the morning for a statement.

On the drive, returning home, we spot three police cars, lights flashing on the side of the road beside an overturned car. I hope it is the loony who hurt Jeo, and I hope he is dead. I want revenge.

Back in my suite, exhausted I fling myself on the bed crying. I blame myself for buying the accursed toy cars that led Jeo to play on the parking lot. I don't think I could stand hearing of his death. That little boy with his mischievous smile opened my heart even more than Robin. Eventually I fall asleep. A slumber plagued with nightmares full of blaring sirens, the impact of tender flesh with gleaming metal, unbearable screams of panic.

At six o'clock I am wandering aimlessly around the room, every part of my body hurts. I have difficulty breathing. My hands are shaking so much that I cannot maintain a glass of water steady. I must take hold of myself for the worst might be to come. I had slept fully dressed; I am taking a shower and I change clothes. Harvey knocks at the door. He is in terrible shape, pale, dishevelled, I don't think he was able to sleep and I am sure he has been drinking. I must take over because he is about to collapse.

"Come Harvey, you cannot leave Morgan all alone. You are going to take a shower, while I prepare coffee. You must eat something too, because it will be a long day. I will take care of Morgan while you go to the hospital. It is no use to go too early because the doctors don't make their rounds that early. Hopefully June will be released today." I lead him back to their apartment. He is like a zombie, I must remember that he is no more than twenty five or twenty six and he has already had a full load of sorrow in his life. He is a very fragile young man. I have a lot of respect for what he has already accomplished. Being the head of a family when you are only seventeen is a very strenuous responsability to swallow for anyone. If he lets me I feel it will be my honour to help in any capacity I can.

We cannot find Morgan, she is not in her bed nor anywhere we search. Finally I scour all the cupboards and find her behind the garbage pail, hugging her stuffed lamb wrapped up in Jeo's batman cape. She does not want to come out. She says she is talking to her brother. I convince her that as soon as she is finished talking we are going to have a swell breakfast together and go for a walk. She asks for 'raiolys' and wants ice cream on a donut for her brother.

Harvey, now cleaned up and fed, has regained some composure. He tells me he called his father and his sister. His father cannot be reached but his sister is coming. They are holding a ceremony for Jeo's welfare. I tell him I will attend with Morgan and that he should not forget to call and let me know what is happening at the hospital. He leaves under Morgan's loud protests.

Alone with the child I start an animated conversation with my coffee spoon.

"Are you going to stir my coffee, or not?" I ask in a belligerent voice.

"No, the coffee is too hot, besides I don't want to get wet." says the spoon pouting.

"Then I am going to call you a lollipop, and I am going to lick you and tickle you all over with my wet tongue." Morgan stops crying, runs to me and declares she wants to lick the spoon. I say "OK" and I put the spoon to my ear. "That spoon is telling me that it wants to be dipped a little in the glass of milk before you lick it. "OK" agrees Morgan giggling. She licks the wet spoon a few times, grabs the glass of milk and drinks it all. Amazing how a child's mood improves when fed.

"Talk some more to the spoon" she says "but after it will be my turn". Ten minutes later she and I try to teach the stuffy lamb to play hopscotch on the table top. We are having a grand time because the lamb is exceedingly dumb. It keeps falling off the table to peals of laughter. Harvey's sister arrives with her four children in tow. She is a sour woman. It is very difficult to have a conversation with her. She seems to be leery of white people. No wonder! Harvey told me that she was raised in a succession of no less than ten different foster homes, some awful and some not so hot. She takes over and tells me that I will not be needed anymore.

Harvey phones; June has had a miscarriage and is still in shock and sedated; the doctor wants to keep her another day or two. During the night Jeo has been flown to a much larger hospital in Vancouver. I tell him that I am going back tomorrow and with his permission I will visit the boy.

I better start packing. I am very tired but mostly anxious. The police call, they want me to make a deposition on what happened to Jeo. They say that the reason the officers did not stop is that they did not see the accident while pursuing a man who was wanted for assaulting someone on a cruise ship. That is the first good news of the day. The third guy I feared, is kaput. May he rot in Hell! I can relax and Cynthia too. I should phone to tell her but I don't have the energy. I tell the officer that I will be at the detachment later this afternoon because I am flying back the day after. I flop on the bed for an agitated nap. Robin's call wakes me up. He wants to have a sandwich with me downtown. I tell him what happened with Jeo. He says he will be coming as soon as he can. He seems very concerned. I don't know if I should tell him about my deal with Tony. Probably I will because I want to keep our relationship free of little secrets.

A timid tap-tap on the door, it is Morgan with a big smile who wants to check if I have more talking spoons. Her aunt is trailing behind, and snaps the girl away with an accusing frown. I don't know how to deal with so much anger and distrust. I long to retreat to my computer, all this aching, this turmoil is taking a toll on me. I must prepare to meet Robin and go to see the police.

Another knock at the door, decidedly I can't rest. I must open it because it could be Harvey with more news. It's a reporter from the local newspaper who wants to ask about the accident. I tell him what he wants to know, telling him that I thought the police were not supposed to chase cars at such a speed. I also blame the ambulance services for not being able to come fast enough. I am in a rotten mood. Drained.

Robin comes next, he has the good sense to hug me really tight and again I start sobbing. He lets me cry for a long time, soothing in a gentle voice. I say that I had something to tell him but I forgot. He says that it is OK and asks if I still want to go for lunch. I am not sure and he says that since it is probable that I have nothing in the fridge it would do me good to get out for a bite.

The restaurant is not very busy; Robin chooses a table far from other diners and orders BLTs and coffee for both of us. He talks of the unusually nice weather for the season, of the upcoming of hunting season and whatnot. Then I remember Tony's offer.

"I can't believe you accepted!" he says horrified.

"The money is good; I could do with a bit more cash." I retort with a lame smile.

"You are the one who told me that money is nothing compare to peace of mind."

"Well, I changed my mind, that's all." Putting an end to the conversation.

Robin is very upset. I actually think that he cares a lot.

"Listen, Robin, I am not like you, I can do it a few times and then claim that I am too sick or that I have a touch of Alzheimer's, or something like that. I will be safe enough, don't worry. Think about it if I do a few runs I could help you with your debts."

"So, you are the one I have to deliver the parcel to at the airport. This Tony is a real devil! He told me that he met a real nice woman; she was a bit of a crackpot but could be useful. I had no idea it was you. The joke is on us. By the way do you want to hear another joke? Guess who delivered buds to me yesterday. Harvey! The four units of the motel that are always empty? I would not be surprised if it was used as a grow-op."

"Sweet Harvey? Are you sure? Now be kind to your poor Auntie, as you call me. One thing at a time, please. Was he just doing an errand and delivering stuff, or was it his own stuff?"

I don't know, I just paid him, the fewer questions you ask and the less you will be lied to. Besides I am not supposed to care."

What did I wish for when I started this 'Now" business? Some excitement. Be careful what you wish for, you might get it said my father when he was in his fatherly mood. All the same I have a knack for falling for deviant characters, I must admit. I am most probably a deviant too if I go by the proverb -Birds of a feather flock together.

Robin drops me off at the police station and we will meet again at the library when I am finished; he will drive me back to the motel. I appreciate the offer because I am not feeling very well. I worry about Jeo. I dread the outcome of the injury just as much as the possibility of his death. It is sucking up all my energy. In a sense I am not unhappy to return home; I need to get my bearings.

At the police station, it is the same officer that Cynthia and I met at the hospital for Macky who is going to take my deposition; she remembers me and wonders why I haven't gone yet. I tell her that I had some more people to see, that Macky is slowly recovering. She confirms that the hit and run motorist died on impact and he was the one who had aggressed Macky. I feel hugely relieved. She says that she is not sure whether he was insured and what happens in terms of compensation for his victim. The hospital told her that Jeo is suffering from a severe head contusion and that they don't have the medical resources to treat him in Prince Rupert.

After Robin drives me back, I dump all my stuff disorderly in my bags and go to bed. I wake up early, my plane leaves at nine AM; I must return the car, pick up my ticket and meet Robin with the parcel. I hope it is not too big and it will fit in my carry-on.

Robin is waiting for me in the airport lobby, he hands me a square brown packet weighing around two pounds; he kisses me and wishes me a nice uneventful trip and say that he will wait until I pass security. I can't get over how he is the spitting image of Edgar. This is something I want to keep secret.

No problems at security. Phew!

Not all the seats are occupied on the plane fortunately because I was assigned one beside a fellow who reeks of old perspiration combined with a whiff of overly cooked fried onions. He must not have taken a shower for a week at least and has poor dental hygiene. When he takes his shoes off, that does it for me, even if it is only a two hour flight I will not endure it. I quickly secure the two seats at the back of the plane near the toilets where I will be able to spread my legs. The space allotted to passengers on planes is getting smaller all the time. I don't know how the six foot tall guys get by; I can barely move. I better forget about crabbing and try to snooze for a while; I don't have a clue as to what is waiting for me in Vancouver.

Back in town

We arrive on time in Vancouver; a young fellow behind me at the luggage carousel asks me if he can help with my luggage, he is a clean cut sort of guy with a goatee, one you would expect to work in a bank or an insurance company. I scan him from the bottom up: good shoes, creased pants, opened-collar fresh pressed shirt, and an honest face. He tells me that he could drive me home if I want; his car is in the parking lot. Then he asks whether I want to use his phone. It's an iPhone or this kind of newest contraption that takes photos, records movies and so forth. Of course I am not too familiar with these new machines since I never had the money to buy one. Not that I would want one, what would I do with it. As I put my hand out to refuse his offer I see my picture is on the screen with Harvey's Paradise in the background. I understand this fellow is my contact for the delivery so I readily accept the ride.

In the black BMW that looks uncannily like the one Tony was driving at the cabin, the fellow smiles a lot but seems to lack the gift of gab. Even when I ask his name, he smiles but remains mute. He helps with my luggage, comes up with me at the apartment, takes the package, asks if my passport is valid and leaves.

I should restock my fridge but first call the hospital to get some news from Jeo; Cynthia can wait. Over the phone I present myself as Jeo's grandmother. Jeo is still in a coma, an operation was performed to release the brain from a haemorrhage. He is in intensive care, resting. I cannot see him yet. The prognosis is not good. I am numb with fear for him and for the family. I must keep active not to let the dread invade me. It is my experience that when I let worries pollute my neuron channels I turn dumber than a door knob. Maybe it is because I go to the 'After' leaving the 'Now' unattended. Not a good scene. So I start by doing some house cleaning. House cleaning is good if you really get into it. Unfortunately my place does not lend itself much to serious scrubbings.

The phone rings pulling me from dusting under the bed. It is June, Harvey in the background. She is frantic. I invite her to come down and stay with me for as long as she needs to while Jeo is hospitalized. She is coming in on tomorrow morning's flight, and yes she can take Morgan along, I will baby sit her while she is visiting the boy. Better that than leaving the child with her sour auntie.

I return to my dusting trying to figure out the sleeping arrangements. I must go to Canadian Tire before it closes to buy a double-size air mattress. While standing on a chair dusting the blades of the ceiling fan I wonder if Cynthia has extra bedding supplies I could borrow and as I don't want to stop my self-imposed house chores I step down from the chair, grab the phone climb right back up and call holding the phone between my ear and my shoulder still scrubbing. The chair is wobbly. Good, it keeps me on my toes. My wits are slowly returning. I am efficiently multitasking in the 'Now'.

Cynthia is not at her best. Macky is suffering something fierce. She exhales a sigh of relief on hearing about the three goons being gone to the Yonder and expresses her concern for Jeo. Yes she has all the bedding I need for June and Morgan. She says she is coming to deliver it herself because she missed me so much. She also wants to go shopping with me for the air mattress; she needs to take a break from nursing Macky. She will be at my place in fifteen minutes waiting in a cab.

In the cab she kisses and hugs me giggling like a school girl, all I hope is that she does not start singing Clementine. She says that Macky is a difficult patient, yet it is true that he suffers a great deal "The Poor Dear". His doctor said that it might take him a good four months to recover. I suggest a celebration of sorts for our deliverance from the baddies. Cynthia reminds me that Macky is taking a lot of pain killers and should definitely not mix it with any alcoholic beverage. So we opt for half a bottle of good Gewürztraminer and a strawberry short cake once we find the air mattress at Canadian Tire. I do not want to talk about Jeo; I am too scared she will say something that I find offensive in my precarious state of mind. Winston the cat is his usual independent self and has disappeared from Macky's apartment this morning. I wonder if he will show up at my place. I prefer not to share my adventures with Robin, and even less with Tony.

Cynthia proposes Macky's car to go pick up June and the child at the airport tomorrow morning. She is sure he would not mind. That is a swell idea especially since I don't know at all if June knows how to find her way in a big city. I am not even sure she has ever been to Vancouver.

At Canadian Tire, the hardware store that prides itself for its large assortment of tools, outdoor and sporting goods, I find the perfect air mattress, thick and cozy enough for two people, I also get an electric pump to blow it up effortlessly and as an afterthought I get a folding screen to give June and me a bit of privacy since she is going to sleep in the living room with Morgan. At the cashier, I proudly produce one of Tony's hundred dollar bills. What a treat for me to look casual about a disbursement, not to search for the last dime to complete a payment, and not to anticipate with dread the pinch I will suffer for weeks to recover from the spree. Lack of financial means can seriously impede freedom of spirit.

The taxi has been waiting for us. We will unload all the stuff at my place and I will treat Cynthia to an ice cream crowned with a delicate wafer served in a real glass dish offered by a polite waitress at a nice table in the salon de thé close by. We will lift our right pinkie and talk niceties about the clement weather we are enjoying so late in the season. Jeo is at the back of my mind but I know that fretting is not going to help him, or me for that matter. I still have to go shopping to stock the fridge so I hope that Cynthia is not going to linger too long on her many problems where Macky takes a most important chunk of the worries now that the goons are nothing but a bad memory.

By the time I have gone shopping for food, and a few toys for Morgan at the Salvation Army, sorted out the bedding, gone down to do my laundry, called the local newspaper to resume delivery and checked out my email I am exhausted. I go lie down with a book; as a rule I find books much more effective than sleeping pills.

I wake at five in the morning full of aches and pains after a very agitated night filled with nightmares where Jeo dies, June in a frenzy strangles me while a one-winged robin flutters about. If I were smart I would do some Tai Chi exercises to get my bearings but I don't have the energy, instead I brew a cup of coffee and take it to bed with the newspaper. Outside the door Winston the cat was sitting on the paper in what I estimate to be a very rude attitude; the blasted cat slipped between my legs to resume its elected hideout under my bed. I am in no mood to chase it.

I must have fallen asleep because it is now nine o'clock so I must rush to have breakfast and prepare to go to the airport. I call Cynthia; she seems to be in a better disposition since she decided last night to undergo a facelift with botox injections. I can come anytime for the car keys, just ring her apartment number. The car is parked in the underground garage, I can keep it as long as I need it Macky is in no condition to drive for a while and she does not drive herself because she has a touch of ocular glaucoma. I tell her the cat is under my bed. Also that she should not hesitate to ask me, in case Macky needs to go to a doctor's appointment, I could drive.

The miracle

At the airport, June is not the serene young mother I first met, she looks pale, her beautiful brown eyes are dulled, she is frightened, on the verge of collapse. The little girl clings desperately to her mother and definitely has no time for me. I plan to drive them directly to the children's hospital and I offer to look after Morgan, but June wants me with her, I think she is too shy to talk to the medical staff by herself. She says that Harvey's father, the shaman, is coming down tomorrow. He wants to hold a healing ceremony for Jeo. This might not be easy to negotiate with the personnel in charge. I dare not ask what it involves and I am not sure June knows either; I better look it up on the internet or maybe call Harvey, he might know.

At the hospital, I stop for a moment at the gift store to get a few fancy candies and small toys as lures for Morgan, because I suppose she will not be allowed near her brother and I will have to keep her quiet. Not a small task considering the mood she is in.

There must be an improvement in Jeo's condition because he has been moved from the intensive care unit to a room by himself in a ward. I suppose that he has been put in isolation because of the mumps. The single room is good news considering the shamanic ceremony tomorrow. June is totally despondent, the little girl holds on to her. The environment frightens them both. Fortunately the head nurse is most pleasant. She is trained to deal with distraught families. June claims me as her Aunt. So since I must look to her as the one that will understand what she has to say she addresses me rather than June.

Jeo is still in a coma, but all his vital functions are restored, he breathes on his own, it is too early to assess the damage to the brain, if any. A doctor should soon come to talk to us. Yes June can go see her son but it is better for Morgan to stay outside. I really can't figure out what is best for me to do: tend to June or to Morgan. The nurse decides for me. She takes the howling child with her and tells us that she will be in the playroom. I am not sure I would have dealt with the problem as authoritatively but who am I to know, me the barren woman? Worse things were done to me as a child and I survived.

We enter Jeo's room, with our face masks, pink sanitized hospital gowns and sterilized rubber gloves, I hold June's waist firmly because I am afraid she will faint. The boy looks so small in his bed; he is hooked up to a saline drip. His leg is in a cast, slightly elevated, his head has been shaved. June's knees buckle under her; she slips from my grip and ends in a heap on the floor. I must admit that looking at this little charming imp of a boy reduced to such a bandaged lump on a bed made my heart miss a beat.

I kneel down beside June and whisper comforting words to her. I tell her that the two of us are going to put Jeo back on his feet. I talk and talk holding her head tight on my lap, caressing her face, my tears wetting her cheeks, and finally she comes to. I tell her to be strong for Jeo, that he needs her. I tell her that the Wolf spirit is with her, and also the Beaver, the Eagle and the Bear. I name all the animal autochthon symbols I have seen on totem poles. Finally she smiles and says: "Granny Clara, you are so funny when you are scared." And there the myth I was told about the stoic Indian is revealed to me as a big hoax.

"I am of the Butterfly clan." She says getting up.

"Oh marvellous, tomorrow Harvey's father is going to dance the Butterfly prayer and Jeo will hear it and feel better."

Harvey's father is not a Butterfly, he is a Frog, I could not have married someone of my own clan."

I have so much to learn and there is so little time. Who would have known that a butterfly and a frog could make such beautiful children?

June is holding Jeo's hand. The doctor comes in. A tall gangly young fellow with long curly hair and big bags under his eyes. He is obviously exhausted. He says that we must be patient; that Jeo might wake up as if nothing happened, but no one knows what damage was done. We should talk to him because he seriously thinks that comatose patients can sometimes hear and understand. I mention that Jeo's grandfather is a shaman. Could we have the permission to perform a ritual in the hospital?

"What does it consist of?" he asks with evident interest.

"I am not sure. I have not known the family that long. I know it means a lot to them" and I explain, leaving some parts of the story in the dark, how I met the family and how I befriended them. I also mention my guilt of being in part responsible for Jeo's accident by offering the toy cars.

The young doctor sits down, he wants to hear more. He claims he has been working a twenty hour shift and is exhausted but is always keen on learning more about his patients whom he only sees when they are unconscious.

"I am an ICU, Intensive Care Unit specialist, so my work is mostly mechanical. My goal is to maintain vital signs in an otherwise mostly unconscious patients. As soon as they are stabilized they are directed to appropriate wards. So my interactions with patients are minimal. I miss out on the social aspect of medicine. My name is Craig. I would very much like to participate in the ritual or if not participate at least witness it. It would be both interesting for me to gauge medically the reaction of the boy as well as meeting a Native chief in the exercise of his function. I have to admit I am grossly ignorant on that level. Anyway I am going to give recommendations at the nurses' desk to allow the ceremony."

I never imagined it would be that easy, I thought I would have so much explanation and pleading to do. I am impressed. Another preconceived idea of mine proved wrong. How long will I have to live to free myself of projecting my own narrowness of mind on to others?

Meanwhile, there is a huge commotion in the hall. Morgan, the little sister, has escaped the playroom where she had been parked and is running wild screaming that she wants to see her brother, NOW. I step out of Jeo's room and she runs into me, hugging my legs, calling me Spoon. That spoon trick I played on her back at the motel must have stuck in her mind.

I whisper in her ear that if we make too much noise some big policemen will throw us out and we won't get raviolis anymore. It's a trick I learned somewhere, when someone screams at you, you are way better off to start whispering instead of shouting back.

She quietens almost instantly, though she is still breathing haltingly.

"If you promise to be extra quiet I will take you to Jeo, you must understand that he is very sick and he is sleeping so we are going to tiptoe to not wake him up. After that we will go to Granny Clara's and look at the toys she bought for you. It is a surprise."

She nods wordlessly sealing the deal. We enter holding hands into Jeo's room as two responsible composed people. The doctor has gone. June is prostrated at the head of the bed, her head resting on Jeo's hand. Morgan screams in that shrill piercing voice of hers: "Mommy, you are going to wake Jeo!"

This is when I witness the miracle. I am sure I saw and heard it. Jeo's lips moved and he said "Turnip". Maybe I am the only one to see it, but my eyes blur, my heart jumps a few beats and nobody is going to take this away from me. I need a chair. Morgan has just proven, at least to me, that she has a say as to what is going on.

A nurse comes in and asks June if she wants to have a cot set up in Jeo's room so she could stay overnight with her child. June looks at me for approval. We step out and I give her my phone number, my address and take her to the hospital cafeteria for some refreshments. I promise I will be back tomorrow with Morgan early in the afternoon to greet the shaman and be part of the ceremony.

I leave with Morgan but not before I whispered in Jeo's ear that I am counting on him to come back fast from where ever he is because I want to go with him to see a lion and a panda at the zoo. I must be off my rocker to promise such a treat when I don't even have a car to take him to the zoo in Seattle. My wrongfully earned money is disappearing very fast. I better go and buy that pair of shoes I promised myself before I return to my end of the month cat food diet or I might end up having to buy one shoe at a time on a thirty-six month instalment plan at a twenty-five percent interest rate. We the poor, we better curtail our needs to the bone. If I purchase the cheapest handbag at Wal-mart and I pay with my credit card it will cost me more than if I bought a Gucci bag cash. By the time I finish paying for it, it will be so worn out that I will need a new one. On and on it goes.

By the time we arrive at my place, Morgan is not in the best of moods. Fortunately the cat is at the door waiting for us. That's welcomed entertainment. The phone light is flashing wildly. A call from Robin, one from Cynthia another from Harvey and another that I don't know whom from.

Cynthia is frantic, Macky had some kind of a seizure and was transported to the hospital by ambulance, the prognosis is not good. She is with him and would like me with her. I am stranded here with Morgan and I can't honour her request. Robin can wait until tomorrow; I call Harvey and let him know what I saw. He says he is arriving on an early flight to be in time for the ceremony with his father and will be returning the same day on the last flight out. Could I come to pick them up? I will do what I can. It is rather late for me to take a crash course on parenting. The scant souvenirs I have of my own childhood are not helping much. I must play it by ear. Morgan and the cat have already broken a vase and spilled milk on the carpet while I was on the phone. Any minute now I am expecting a knock on my door from the tenant downstairs inquiring about the noise.

I lie flat on my back on the side of the carpet that is not wet with milk, I lift my legs up straight and start singing "Ommmmmm". Morgan stops running around:

"What are you doing?"

"I am singing to the ceiling to see if the fairies are going to dance for me."

"I want to do that too."

"You have to be very quiet, and do just like I do. Close your eyes and check if you see any fairies."

The cat jumps on my stomach and paws my shirt methodically.

"I don't see anything."

"That's too bad, because I see one right near the light; she has a green skirt, yellow eyes and fancy little red shoes with a pompom." I whisper.

She catches on. "Mine is all blue with purple hair." She whispers back "She is hanging by the 'curtin' and holds Jeo's hand."

"I guess she is going to make him feel better."

"Yes, "she says "in two sleeps he will be all better."

"I think we should eat something nice, then put our PJs on and watch a nice cartoon on TV, the cat can watch too. How about that?"

She is all for it. She hugs me tight "I like you Granny 'Cara'"

So far, so good, I am on the winning side. I still fear the going to bed issue. Will she want her mother? I will address the problem when it arises. I fear the tears, the tantrums, the feeling of abandonment.

We eat a bowl of chicken soup; dip some crackers in a tuna fish dip, and finish with an ice cream sandwich. Then we settle on my bed, the three of us to be lulled by the Pink Panther's antics on the Family Channel. I made sure I disconnected the telephone so as not to be disturbed. We fall asleep just like that.

I wake up at midnight, go check my email in the living room, put the phone back on the receiver and plug it back in its socket, make myself a piece of toast, but I soon lie on the air mattress I had prepared for June because I will need all my wits early in the morning. We must go to the airport to pick up Harvey and drive him to the hospital. I think I will leave the little girl with him for the day. I need time for myself. This babysitting job is exhausting also I have some other business to attend to. What with Macky in the hospital and Robin who did not sound too well on the phone and what about this anonymous call. I hope it is only a marketing call about a most undesirable product. The deal of the century where I would only have to give my credit card number just to pay for the shipping cost to receive free of charge a set of self cleaning oven mitts. They would be mailed to me today direct from Bangladesh.

The phone wakes me up, I try to reach my clock radio, and I roll off the air mattress I had forgotten that I was sleeping in the living room. It's seven thirty, and it's Harvey calling from the airport in Prince Rupert. He does not need me to pick him up at the airport, his father will be there. I can join him later at the hospital. The phone call woke Morgan up. She is probably afraid as she finds herself in unfamiliar surroundings and is silently crying for her mother. She does not want raviolis for breakfast, so I suggest triple chocolate donuts and she perks up. We dress up singing "head, shoulders, knees and toes, knees and toes..." I impress myself with my kindergarten savvy but I will have to switch songs very soon for the limbering exercise so early in the morning will kill my poor back. I feel no express need to visit my toes at daybreak. The hair brushing is a complicated ordeal but we get through it in decent shape. The cat wants out; it is just as well since we are all set to be on our way to the donut factory nearby.

On the opposite sidewalk I notice a fellow that I think I recognize. As his face slowly comes back to me I have no intention to acknowledge him. That is the same guy who came to drive me home from the airport. The reason I did not place him at once is that he is not wearing the same outfit he wore when I first met him. He is sporting a jogging suit, a tuque and from the looks of it some very expensive running shoes. He crosses the street at a trot and falls in step with us.

"Why didn't you call me back?"

"I cannot talk to you now; I am busy as you can see. We are on our way to get some donuts."

"You are expected to be ready at all times."

"I was not told anything of the sort."

"Are you a mule or not?"

A mule? I have not been called that since childhood, by my mother as a matter of fact whenever I was not compliant enough for her tastes. I find that offensive coming from that young fellow who otherwise had been very polite the first time I met him. And then it strikes me that it is the term these people commonly use for their carriers. So I calm down before I put him in his place.

"Don't you have a cell?" he asks.

"Certainly not, do you think I am made of money?"

He shrugs, "Take this one and make sure you answer it. Don't use it unless you are told to do so." And to my relief he jogs away from us. I am not sure anymore whether I want to get involved. I will call Tony as soon as I am alone to tell him I quit. I will return the money he gave me. I am glad I did not spend it all; I am still on Cynthia's money.

"Who was that man" Morgan asks "I don't like him." perceptive this little girl.

"I am not sure I like him either; let's go eat." I reply offhandedly.

After the donut and the glass of milk we feel restored enough to loiter some in the big mall; visit the toy department at Walmart and even buy a plastic miniature horse mounted by an Indian chief in full regalia, feathers and all for the mere sum of nine ninety nine. It is now time to get back to the garage, get the car and drive to the hospital.

The cell phone rings. A male voice orders me to be at the bus depot at three this afternoon. Someone will meet me there. The connection is cut off before I can reply. I am starting to feel very jittery. I long to be bored like I was a month ago. A boring life is good. I am starting to blame the cat and my rotten luck.

I am not sure I want to be in the "Now" anymore. The "Then" I can manage easily, I always give it a little twist to suit my mood of the moment. Who is going to blame me? Big serious respectable history books are reinvented all the time. That's how sometimes Edgar is the handsome affectionate lover, and other times the sniveling luckless cad while at other times the messed-up rotten gambler. My mother the smiling brainless blonde or the accepting corporate wife whose function is to entertain and shut up; but when I am in a forgiving mood she can also be the victim of the society in which she grew up; for she was not stupid and she warned me often not to follow in her path. My father the learned barrister, the lecherous idiot or the nice guy who could invent funny games when he was trying to apologize for not being the attentive parent. During recollection, all this cast of characters represents I guess some of the many facets of the person I review through my kaleidoscopic mind glasses. I think the coloring has to do with the environment of the moment. I am a long way away from the serenity I am supposed to have reached with age.

My emotions play tricks on me. My present, my "Now" tints the setting of my "Then" and its characters follow suit switching from malicious villains to benevolent fools even reaching the state of adorable puppets when I feel all mushy. I am however painfully aware that these people actually existed and are by no means rightfully represented in my private replays. The characters displayed are nothing but a reflection of me onto them, an evidence of my shortcomings. If I wake up with an upset stomach, a back pain or even an ingrown toenail these people turn vicious. On a rainy day they are just fools but when I smell the roses and I just received my pension cheque, I love them all.

While I was mulling this over Morgan was singing at the top of her voice:"If you're happy and you know it; clap your hands…"to the plastic brave we just bought, we have reached the hospital ward. It is amazing, when administered judiciously, what a donut and the appropriate trinket can do to your overall outlook on life. For myself, I am not sure whether even a dozen donuts and a new pair of shoes would do the trick. I dread entering Jeo's room. If this little boy does not get better I will be devastated. The boy has stolen my heart and I feel guilty to have been instrumental in the accident.

Maybe to delay looking at Jeo I stop by the head nurse's desk. She is a petite harassed woman in her mid-fifties. She greets me amiably with what I detect as a touch of condescension.

"The boy from the report I read this morning has had a very agitated night."

"Is that good or bad"

"I could not tell, you would have to talk to the doctor who treats him. We might have to remove the mother from his bedside. Your daughter is exhausted and might disturb the patient."

She must think I am the head of the tribe, my blue eyes and pale skin only being a positive result of residential school whose supreme indoctrination mandate was and I quote again "to kill the Indian in the child".

"Did the doctor, I forgot his name, make provision for the ceremony the grandfather, the shaman, is going to perform?" I ask.

"I don't know a thing about that, but if it does not make noise or prevent us from tending to the patient medically, you may go ahead. At my age and with my experience in this hospital you can bet that I have seen it all." She says dismissively.

I sense that I should be extremely careful not to antagonize this woman; she could be a formidable adversary. I try to break the ice with her.

"I imagine that in a big hospital like this one you must see all kinds of going-ons." I say in a confidential tone.

"You would not believe! Only last week people brought a football to a recently leg amputated boy whose life expectancy was less than a year. I caught a mother smuggling junk food to her grossly obese child, and right now there is a party of praying women cluttering your grandchild's room. So a horde of feathered dancing Indians will only bring more atmosphere to an otherwise boring ward. But if the doctor gave his approval, who am I to oppose…" she says belligerently.

It is interesting to notice that even I who have always taken pride in my meek efforts to unconventional thinking and living would have leaned toward her pragmatic outlook. All we need now is a bunch of Tibetan monks with their praying wheels to turn the willfully aseptic ambiance of the hospital into a holistic circus. But this was all before I met Jeo. Deep down I am convinced now that if Jeo is going to get better; it is through magic. So I would welcome the Tibetan monks with opened arms and I am going to kick out the praying biddies who in my books welcome tragedies. So I whisper in Morgan's ear: "You and I, we are going to make Jeo better." Then I take her hand and we march to the sick child's room. We are on the war path.

June embraces me sobbing on my shoulder, Harvey is in a corner seething, the shaman is preparing his paraphernalia, and Morgan is bracing my legs tight, the head biddy comes to me: "Jesus loves you my dear" she says in a mellow voice.

"If you will excuse us, my Dear, we need a little family time, here. So if you don't mind I would appreciate if you would quietly leave the room for a while. I understand you mean well but privacy to us Tsimshians is of the utmost importance in this trying time."

She summons her partners with an angelic smile, and they leave. The shaman winks at me. I lead June to Harvey and Morgan and I approach Jeo's bed. Morgan jumps on the bed and snuggles against her brother amid the various life supporting tubes plugged into his poor body.

I lean towards him, I have decided that I must ally with the children; they are the ones who understand magic. I hold both children's hands; we form a circle of strength. I am tempted to shout Abracadabra. "Hey, Muscle man, you better wake up soon, because I have tickets to go to the zoo; see lions, and zebras and monkeys. Forget school for a while. This is Granny Clara, have I ever lied to you? I know you can hear me." There goes what is left of Tony's money. I am stuck being a mule. Am I wishful thinking? I feel pressure coming from Jeo's hand. Morgan has closed her eyes "You are my big brother!" she shouts and June faints. The shaman intones a rhythmic humming sound. Harvey lies June on the cot. The good doctor comes in accompanied by two nurses and three men in white coats. I hope it is not to take us all to the loony bin. One nurse attempts to rush to June while the other is clearly aiming at Morgan. The doctor, may the likes of him live forever, stops them both. The shaman is now in a trance, he circles the bed. It all appears as in slow motion. I hold my breath but again I feel Jeo's hand. This time I am sure he is responding I dare not move. I feel like screaming but it is Harvey who lets out the most commanding howling sound, the calling of the Alpha wolf.

The head nurse shows her head through the door:"What the hell is going on in here?" and Jeo, my dear, my cute, my beloved little boy opens his eyes and says in a perfectly clear voice: "Let's get out of here. I am thirsty." If I don't sit I will collapse, my heart is pounding so hard against my chest. I knock on Jeo's leg. "That hurts!" he says. I am laughing hysterically. The shaman keeps drumming. The doctor checks Jeo's pulse. The nurses are tending to June. Morgan is jumping up and down on the bed. "That's him!" she says brandishing the plastic brave on his also plastic horse "I told him to do it."

We won, we won, we won!

After I explain to the doctor that June had a miscarriage only three days ago, he recommends rest, and gives her a sedative. Harvey is going to stay overnight and leave on the earliest flight tomorrow morning. June comes back to my place. Morgan wants to stay with her brother. I will bring June back to the hospital later this evening if I can. I must tend to my mulish business if I don't want to end up in a dump with a bullet in my head. At least not before I go to the zoo. Outside the Christian ladies are celebrating on their knees the success of their prayers. I thank them profusely.

It is noon now, I have installed the much sedated June on my bed, leaving her with a set of keys to my apartment, and a ten dollar bill to call a taxi to go back to the hospital if I am not back. I also leave written instructions on the dining room table in case she forgets what I just told her. She falls asleep crying.

The mule

I call Cynthia to inquire about Macky. She is still at his bedside, there is little improvement on his condition and the doctors are less than optimistic. I tell her I will be with her as soon as I can but for the moment I have urgent business to tend to. I send her my love and head toward the bus depot by sky train. I do not want Macky's car to be identified and I want to be there a little ahead of time to survey the place. I wear a tuque and sunglasses because that's what I think hoodlums normally wear according to my flimsy knowledge of illicit activities. I raise my shoulders, stick my chin out, and walk with hands in my pockets, legs slightly apart like I saw the toughies do streaming out of high school. I don't feel very comfortable and I swear to myself that this is the last of my larks in hoodlumery, I am clearly out of my league.

At the bus depot I do not spot anything out of the ordinary. A young man joins me in my perambulations. An ordinary type of chap, dressed in outdoorsy Vancouverite garb; so plain that you would not recognize him in a crowd. "I had a hard time spotting you" he says "why did you dress like a clown? Remove this tuque and sunglasses immediately, don't act anything out of the ordinary just like a dumb old broad. It should not be too hard. This is why you have been chosen, because of your looks. If I tell a certain someone how you showed up; he is going to get very mad."

This young upstart is not giving me instructions; I believe he is reprimanding me. Like a superior to an underling. I am not sure how to deal with that. I have little tolerance for hierarchic structure. I have always been self-employed and the people I sometimes could afford to hire I considered them as co-workers. They were supposed to work with me not for me. I opt to shut up and I remove the tuque; of course my hair is a mess.

He gives me a key to a locker; I am supposed to get what's inside. "Handle it with gloves. Don't leave your finger prints on it. It is labeled to Homer Hutchison a friend of yours. Don't worry he is dead. You will leave the luggage in the bus luggage compartment… "

I hope you didn't forget your passport".

"No, no it's in my inside pocket."

"At least that!" he sighs "Buy a ticket to Seattle and get off the bus at Bellingham. This is the key to the Bellingham locker where you will deposit the suitcase and take the one that's in the locker, they are identical. Board the bus to Linden; once there wait in the coffee shop. Someone will take you to Abbotsford across the border. You are on a shopping trip and you met a friend in Bellingham who offered you a ride. At a factory outlet you bought a shirt for yourself and some toys for kids you know. Act casual and don't forget you are on a trial run. Go get yourself a woman's magazine and circle in red the front page; carry it at all times. That's how you will be recognized. An old hag with a dumb magazine"

This fellow is definitely a boost to my ego. He hugs me and kisses me good bye as if he were a close relation of mine, the impudent lurch. I am so humiliated but mostly petrified that I dare not rebuke. Then I think about the promised trip to the zoo and my resolution is strengthened. I am going to go through with the ordeal; just for the money.

The suitcase in the locker is so heavy that I need to have someone help me to lift it off. Fortunately it has wheels. I should have bought my fare and the magazine before getting to it. Now I am stuck lugging it around until I board the bus. I need to call Cynthia to tell her that I will not be able to meet her later this evening because I don't know when I will be back. I don't want her to phone my place in case she would wake June up who needs the rest. Of course I cannot use the cell phone I was given so I call from a pay phone. Cynthia is crying, she needs me badly, she says. She does not think Macky is going to make it through the night. I feel bad for the poor wreck and I wish I could be there to at least hold Cynthia's hand. My adventurous spirit has completely disappeared.

I dream of my lonely long walks on the seawall yet I must keep on the Now with all my wits, for I sense that I am on a dangerous path. The young punk talked about trial runs. What if I deliberately failed, would I be, politely or not, excluded? Remembering what happened to the three goons lately I have misgivings. Judging by my physical conditions I could still count on a few more years wandering down the road of the clueless, but this latest endeavor might cut that pretty short. Not that I mind dying but I'd rather do it quietly in my bed and in perfect health with a wise parting word or two. Something with deep meaning like "hasta la vista" or "see you later". I am bragging again, really passing on scares me just as much as anybody else; not so much death itself but the act of dying. I saw a few people give up the ghost and it did not seem very easy for most of them. It took my mother and my grandmother days of agony. So maybe the goon's way with a bullet in the head is the best solution after all.

"You don't travel light." remarks the bus driver lifting the suitcase loading it in the luggage compartment.

"Sorry, it is not mine really, it is my cousin's who passed away and I am returning the stuff he left at my place to his wife. Mostly books."

There is only one seat left on the bus, beside a middle aged woman with a fancy hairdo. She greets me anxious to chat. I welcome the diversion. She claims to be a member of the yacht club in Lacooma; she is out on a spree. She has inside information on the best stores to haunt and is willing to share it with me on a strictly confidential basis. She shows me a pair of gloves she got last month for a mere two hundred bucks. I wonder if I could snatch them from her to handle the suitcase.

We haven't rolled ten miles before she imparts that her husband left her for a younger woman, the bastard, but she has an amazing lawyer and she is going to take him to the cleaners. I would not want to be in her claws. Well, tough luck for the poor jerk. She says her friend is waiting for her in Bellingham with the car, in case I want to join them I am welcome. I politely decline telling her that I too am supposed to meet a friend. She is not put out and "the more the merrier" she says. She won't let go so as a last resort I tell her there was a death in the family and I must spend some time alone with my friend. She commiserates holding my hand truly feeling the loss herself. I will have to console her soon. Meanwhile we have reached the border, I am so tense and frightened that I feel my jaws lock. We must leave the bus and line up to present our passports while the luggage is pulled out of the bus for inspection. Two dogs accompany the customs officers. Jennifer, the name of the fancy hairdo, is chatting away talking about a dog she lost last year and how she still feels the pain. The custom officer smiles at me and hand me back my passport. We are boarding the bus again, the luggage is being loaded back up. Sweat is pouring down my back. The bus leaves, I dare not breathe until we are truly on the highway towards Bellingham.

"You look awfully pale, My Dear" says Jennifer, "would you like a little something to lift your spirit" and with a big grin she puts her finger to her lips; pulls a mickey out of her large purse. I take a big gulp.

"There" she says "I don't mind if I do too."

The stuff is like fire going down my throat; it's pure gin, but she is right, it helps.

"Don't fret I have more, take as much as you want" and she almost finishes the bottle. Some drunks can guzzle a lot before they go right off the bend. She burps not-too-ladylike and falls asleep. I am not used to strong liquor. My head is floating a few inches from the roof of the bus. I feel good, a bit dizzy but all is well in the best of worlds. I don't need to go to a zoo, I am in one.

Getting off the bus in Bellingham I pick up the overweight suitcase with one of Jennifer's two hundred dollar gloves that I had snatched while she was asleep and go to the locker as indicated, the locker is on the second level so I have to ask a nice fellow passing by to lift it up for me, after I have retrieved the one that is in the locker. The new one is very light so I get back to Jennifer who is still in the lobby, waiting for her friend I guess and return the one glove to her. She is all over me, calling me her best friend ever and asking me for lunch next week. I accept since I don't know her address and she does not have mine either; the world is still a perfect place as far as I am concerned.

There is a bus leaving for Linden in ten minutes, if I rush I might be able to catch it. I forgot that I need to pay with US dollars, but there is an ATM in the lobby so, no problems. That reminds me that I still haven't paid my rent. I have never been late before, I always pay as soon as I receive my pension cheque; I don't want to give any reason to the landlord to evict me.

I am famished but there is no time to get a fast snack, I remember now that I have not had anything to eat since the donut with Morgan. To make matters worse there is a fellow sitting next to me who is munching on a big sandwich. I must look desperate because he pulls an apple out of his satchel and offers it to me. This is the most delicious apple I have eaten in a long time. My cell phone rings. On the other end, somebody tells me to say "Hello, Robert"; I comply.

"Are you on the bus to Linden? Answer: I missed the bus or I am on the bus to Linden"

"I am on the bus to Linden"

"Right, you will be picked up as scheduled, bye"

"Bye." I hang up

"My nephew; he thinks he is a big shot because he drives a truck." I tell the apple guy who is just pulling another huge sandwich out of his bag and wipes his hands on the side of his pants. My mouth is watering.

He points at the cell phone and says:"Those things are a real pain in the ass, if you don't mind my saying so, since I got one the wifey is forever on my back, "bring me that, don't forget that, have you called my mother?" And on and on. I am a nice enough guy, but she drives me nuts. Are you polish or something? My wife's mother is, she don't speak too good. My name is Buck Simpson" splattering bread crust on my face he hands me his paw to shake.

"Very nice to meet you Buck, I am Carolane Dubuc." I say wiping my face. I am part of the underworld now and I must not divulge my name to anyone.

"Oh whoa, you are a Frenchie, I thought so. You don't look like anything from these parts. I like Frenchies, they OK 'cept one, the lousy bastard took my job. I told him slow because he don't speak English like we do, so I told him: Look bastard, you're lucky on account that I am a nice guy but you do that to sum other guy and you're going to find yourself in a ditch sumwhere with no more teeth, if you get my drift. You know what he did? Well he just grin', that's all, dumb Frenchie. It's like my in-law coming from the Polsky's land where they don't speak the same English over there. But I have to hand it to her she makes good sausages." Buck might not be the sharpest knife in the drawer but when it comes to sharing apples he is the best.

I like bus rides. Buck and I part best friends. I rush to the little coffee shop for a bit of a snack to-go, I don't know when my ride will show up. I realize that I forgot my Glamour magazine somewhere between Bellingham and Linden. I need to carry it to be identified by the fellow who will drive me across the border. I try to find a place where I could get another but all I can find is the Enquirer, I would have to go elsewhere in town but I dare not leave the place. I borrow a red felt pen from the waitress and I circle the boobs of the she-alien-monster who just landed plump in Arizona direct from an unknown planet in the galaxy. I feel like a bigot for often you can read scoops in the Enquirer months before it becomes news anywhere else; that's because they seldom bother documenting their stories.

I am wolfing down my oily BLT sandwich wondering how long I will have to wait for the ride back home. It is now six thirty and I wish I could phone Cynthia for the latest news on Macky. I am also musing on Robin's tone of voice on the answering machine, he sounded worried. I feel bad that I did not return his call. Fancy that, all these people who have invaded my privacy lately, all because of a crazy willful cat. I will not be back home before nine and by then I will be so exhausted that I won't be much good to anyone let alone myself.

I look out through the window of the little noisy coffee shop. It is pouring rain outside and getting pretty dark. I cannot distinguish the faces of car drivers coming in or taking off. It seems that one is beckoning to me but I am not sure, I hesitate to run through the rain to check. The driver is insistent, he is waving frantically and comprehensibly reluctant to leave the car. I put the now very light suitcase on top of my head to avoid getting wet and go out to check. I am impatient to get back home.

"Are you dense or what? Get in the back seat, fast and shut up!" he says.

Should I, shouldn't I. A second of light soul searching decision. The fellow sounds very much like the fat head who gave me instructions at the bus depot earlier this afternoon. I get in struggling with the suit case. Even before I close the door the car screeches out of the parking lot accompanied with a string of not so mild expletives.

The front passenger has a fancy hairdo, the lacquer sparkling under the street light. We leave the lighted area and engage in what seems to be a country road, dusk and the pouring rain make things difficult to discern. Content to be sheltered in this foul weather and hopefully on my way home I remain quiet. I believe I fell asleep because I had a vivid dream. I keep my eyes closed; the headlights glare of counter traffic is disturbing. Back to the dream. Tony, the suave don appeared to me, I recognized him instantly by the massive gold rings on his fat fingers and his expensive shoes. Shoes are an issue with me. He was wearing a pilot's cap planted jauntily on his head with a name printed in gold, except the name was not 'Tony' but 'Now'. He was kind of floating in an oversized psychedelic t-shirt and the word 'CROCK' in fancy lettering was flashing on and off.

Where is the message? I ponder. Then I recall the Baker's wife, in "Into The Woods", the musical by Sondheim, the most amazing American lyricist and composer singing:

CENTER start

Oh, if life were made of moments,

Even now and then a bad one --!

But if life were made of moments,

Then you would never know you had one.

CENTER end

If there is someone who has an inkling of multi-dimensions in the artist's world of today, it's him.

That here and now stuff I got hooked on is for the birds. I have had it with living in the "Now". I want my life to be a story, sometimes entertaining, sometimes boring. I want it intertwined with the then and the all-is-possible after. I want to rely on the continuity. I am not ready to let go of the past especially if it is going to help me make wiser choices and orient my after. My experience or the lack of it makes me the person I am. I have no desire to be a fluttering idiot angel. Besides, I never know which 'Me' is in the 'Now'. Is it the sprite old girl ambling along the seawall on a sunny day, the cocky vain know-it-all, the hungry or tired hag? There are so many

'Mes'. "Breathe deeply a few times and no matter which 'Me' you are in at the moment; you are going to rejoin the 'I', the true and only 'I'" it says in the Book. Who cares. I enjoy too much wallowing in my emotions to let go of them willingly. Crap on the exclusive "Now". There I said it and I feel better.

It seems to me that we have been driving for some time, while the border from Linden into Canada should only have taken a moment. Ensconced in my cocoon, the suitcase on my knees, I am not going to ask.

The young oaf in the driver's seat is raving against Tony's choice of mules; he is not addressing me so I gather he is directing his invectives at Hairdo. This guy must have serious unresolved issues with his mother. I feel like bashing him one right in his nozzle. I suddenly wake up with a jolt, Hairdo, that's whatever her name was, the woman who chatted with me so jollily on the first bus ride, the two-hundred dollar pair of gloves. She is in it too. Is this a small world or what?

"Hello, My Dear, you had a little snooze; I gather."

I better look casual, nothing out of the ordinary, just a small irrelevant coincidence. I won't even make any signs of recollection.

"My young friend, here, is going to be late for an important date, because he had to come pick me up since this other fellow who was assigned to do the pick-up has had a hitch at the border. Don't worry, we are in good hands. We thought it would be better to re-enter Canada through the same point we came out." She winks. Actually I am not sure she winked, since from where I sit I can only see her left eye.

At the border there are long waiting lines of Canadian shoppers with their strong dollars. Hairdo and I feel a bit embarrassed to shoot the breeze with the oaf in such a belligerent mood. We just make sporadic little hushed comments accompanied by hostile "humphs" from the brute.

The crossing is a formality. We only bought for less than a hundred dollars, so we are cleared in seconds.

"Let me off at the first sky train station on the way, I will manage." I say anxious to be away from such hostility.

Oh, no My Dear, Bill is going to let us both off downtown where his date is waiting and we will take a taxi home from there. You will leave the suitcase in the car. Also let me not forget, I have an envelope for you."

With all my internal ramblings, I had almost forgotten why I had engaged in that unpleasant lark. Money! The zoo!

Vancouver is true to its meteorological predictions. It is raining cats and dogs. We board a taxi. Jennifer, now I remember, that's Hairdo's name, slips the envelope in my hand.

"You deserve it, "she says and then adds "so I gather you have met Tony."

"Yes, I met him recently, as a matter of fact. Do you know him?"

"Oh, yes he is a dear friend of ours. A neighbour you could say. A gem of a fellow, and he takes good care of his people. You will see, now that you are an official part of the organization. I run a few errands for him, now and then. Nothing to it, and I do so love shopping, if you get my meaning! I am sure we will meet again. You see this time I was only there to make sure you did not get all mixed up with these darned hush, hush instructions. It gets complicated once in a while. Pray tell the taxi driver where you want to be dropped off. I figure you live close to the sea, while I live up on the mountain. So you get off first. Don't bother with the fare; I will take care of that."

I give my rightful address to the taxi driver; I have no reason to be discreet, since I think that Jennifer knows more about me than I do about her. I had no idea that the world of trafficking could be so genteel. Had I not been a witness to the ruthless killings in the restaurant I would almost be taken in.

Twice widowed

Facing the entrance to my apartment building, I stop. The blasted cat is waiting. Poor devil he must be hungry and disoriented as much as I am. I should go up and feed him, then make myself a nice cup of tea and jump into bed with a good book, something easy like a whodunit with Miss Marpole discovering a skeleton in her closet or under the grand piano and with her renowned flair finds the cleaver under her bed. The cook's way to leave a clue. Exactly my idea for an alternative to over-the-counter sleeping pills. But I don't know who is upstairs squatting in my digs; June, my swooning Pocahontas, Harvey, the gentle tough guy, the shaman and his drum, not forgetting Morgan, my co-exorcist. I have half a mind to spend the night in a hotel, nearby. Then I remember poor Cynthia and her predicaments tending Macky's last hours. I take the bus to Macky's hospital. It's only a few blocks away but I feel lazy. Besides I just renewed my monthly pass, so I might as well use it.

At the back of the bus there are four loud Asian teenage girls giggling while sipping the largest container of McDonald's sugary colourful concoctions. They are dressed ostentatiously mod and of course inappropriately for the weather. One wears golden sandals laced up to the middle of her plump calves, the other three wear flip-flops, skirts that look more fitting for the stage in a performance of "Swan Lake" and flashy hair clips. The problem is that these girls also show distinct signs of bulimic tendencies and harbour an interesting array of pimples all over their face. This type of style in our part of the country is commonly referred to as Bling-Bling, which means awkwardly and above all unbecomingly flashy. It is particularly prevalent among newly arrived young Asian women. These girls are sent to us by their rich parents to learn English in the flourishing business of language schools sprouting everywhere in British Columbia. They arrive with generous stipends and loiter at downtown McDonalds, pizza parlours and clothing stores. They must be having a ball and I guess are not terribly anxious to return to their countries of origin to get married off to advantageous parties with the main purpose of generating a male offspring. Bling-Bling is not good, bling-bling is poor taste, bling-bling is zero-couth; I am sure Cynthia strongly disapproves of bling-bling. If we could travel back in time and show up only fifty years ago, wouldn't we ourselves be bling-bling then? So maybe these girls are just a bit ahead of their time, and what they are wearing will be the norm very soon, pimples included. As a matter of fact pimples would be a must. If by misfortune and a wrong diet you happened to be free of blemishes you would have to fake some with clever make-up not unlike the marchionesses of the eighteen century who patched a fake beauty spot somewhere on their cheek as the absolute height of fashion. Obesity would also be trendy. We are getting there already with over a third of our population overweight. We will then not be bling-blings anymore but spotty blimp-blimps.

My tiredness is reflecting on my thoughts or it is the opposite? I dread this visit to the hospital for a good bye to poor Macky so I try to divert myself with extraneous thoughts.

Cynthia spots me coming out of the elevator, runs into my arms and starts sobbing on my shoulder. She is probably looking more exhausted than I am. We sit in the hall, holding tight. Even if we have known each other for less than a month, it is true that I feel a strong connection to her; not unlike I suppose soldiers must feel toward their companions in dangerous missions. We will never be the same people we were.

After she recovers some, she blows her nose, wipes her face, straighten her skirt and for good measure dabs a bit of lipstick although somewhat crookedly; she is ready to talk.

"Where were you, Clara? I missed you so much."

"Some day, I might be able to tell you, but for the moment I don't want to embarrass you with irrelevant details. Just know that I had very unpleasant business to tend to. Hopefully it is over and I am with you now; that's what counts. Why aren't you at Macky's bedside?"

"Oh, Clara it is so sad! Macky, so the doctors say has only a few more hours. He does not suffer so much physically because he is on heavy doses of morphine, but he is very aware. Yesterday, I called his former partner, the one who left him. He came and spent a few hours with him. It did not go well. Afterward Macky asked me to call his notary. He wanted to change his will. I know for a fact that he is leaving his car to you. He knows how much you enjoy driving it."

I react with a jolt. A car! Is he crazy or what?

"Please, don't let him do that! I can't afford it! What with the insurances and the parking fees it would break my budget! It's an expensive new car. That would be a poisonous gift to me. So please, please put a stop to it. Plus I would have to pay taxes on it."

"I did not think of that, let me go inside and tell him."

I am pacing the floor. I think of the stupid cat and I am ready to strangle it with my own hands. Macky is looped on morphine, he does not think straight. I hope Cynthia is capable of changing his mind. But I could sell the car and use what is left of the money to buy the pair of shoes I wanted.

"Think fast, Clara. Cool off. Have a drink of water."

Cynthia is waving to me, Macky wants me in. She purses her lips, and seems very excited. Macky is propped up on pillows; his ashen face already shows the mask of death. Smiling he bids me to approach with a movement of his heavily ringed finger.

"He can't speak loudly." Cynthia whispers.

"Hello, my darling little vixen, I have the honour to ask you to be my wife." My eyes must have sprung out of their sockets. This is the last utterance I expected. I turn questioningly to Cynthia and the notary who are grinning beatifically. Poor Macky is high on something, I swear.

"That would solve a lot of estate problems," the bespectacled notary says. "It was my idea." He adds contentedly.

"Please, Darling Clara, say yes" pleads Cynthia.

I am stunned. "Have the three of you gone out of your minds?" I blurt.

"Not at all," replies the conniving man of law "as his rightful wife you would have total privilege of Mr. Fairmount's estate, tax free. You see Mr. Fairmount has no family, in his former will he had bequeathed his entire estate to his partner of many years, but in the light of what he learned from him today; he decided that it would be absolutely inappropriate, so he thought that you might as well enjoy it. "

I turn to Macky "Why don't you marry Cynthia? She has been a friend of yours for quite a while; we hardly know each other."

"I have been married four times, MyDear, and I am very well provided for. You, on the contrary, are experiencing difficulties from what I understand. You are a true friend to me. Believe me when I say reliable friends are hard to come by. You are so clever and know so much. We would be neighbours, you see."

No, I don't see. Macky is grabbing me by the seam of my pants. I bend over him.

"I would like to have someone remember me, and possibly shed a tear or two over my grave."

"But I would anyhow shed tears over you, Macky. You are a brave soul and the world will not be the same without you. You are a kind wonderful man."

"And you are a clever, witty woman that I am glad to have met. Please accept my last request. I wish you the best last years of your life. Hurry up, say yes; I don't have much time left."

Me, stupid me, mushy me, starts crying.

The notary is on his cell phone. Cynthia is embracing me. I am speechless and I can't stop sobbing.

"Have you got a credit card number? I need it for the marriage license, it costs one hundred dollars. I also need your date of birth and your driver's license." Asks the notary who is still on the phone.

Cynthia offers her Visa card.

The notary steps out of the room dialing another number. I hold both Macky and Cynthia's hands. I am completely overwhelmed.

The notary comes back in. "Everything is arranged. A marriage commissioner will be here in twenty minutes, I have your marriage license number. It pays to have connections. Cynthia and I are the witnesses." he says with a self-satisfied smirk.

"You have time to fix yourself up a bit." says Cynthia never forgetting decorum.

"No," says Macky "she is exactly how I want to take her with me. Hard and soft at the same time. Do not change anything, Clara; I like you the way you are. Believe me, if I had not had other inclinations I would have been glad to be your dutiful husband. Nature has arranged it otherwise. I don't regret anything."

Cynthia is beside herself with excitement, she goes back and forth from the window to the door then the bed. I must admit it is difficult to sort one's emotions.

The notary is notary-like, composed, discreet, in full command of the situation. Do I notice his purple socks, or his pink tie? Not me. I, who am soon to be travelling alone on my honeymoon. I am berserk. I repeat to myself that I am just complying with the last will of a poor unfortunate devil; I still feel like a swindler.

The jolly marriage commissioner arrives. She assesses the situation and takes what she thinks is an attitude of circumstances, solemn and non-committal. Cynthia and the notary on both sides of the bed hear Macky and I pronounce the famous:"I do." We will or rather I will receive the marriage certificate by mail.

Macky seems exhausted. His breathing is but a wisp. He is holding both Cynthia's and my hands. The notary leaves with the marriage commissioner, so does Macky not long after with his last words "I could not help it." The nurse arrives. Do I detect a reproachful glance toward me? The doctor arrives and asks me if I have made arrangements. I am baffled but Cynthia takes over. I hear her say that everything is under control. I am now twice widowed. As soon as legal matters are clear, I think I am going to Rio on Macky's money and dance my sadness away; I'll take Cynthia with me.

It is past midnight when we finally leave the hospital, hand in hand and hire a cab to Cynthia's place.

It's the first time I am back here since the cleaning lady masquerade a few weeks ago. So much has happened since then. I am not the same person. I have an odd feeling of being in some kind of lousy whodunit and in a rush to read the last page. I better prepare two cups of tea and put Cynthia to bed. I desperately need to be alone to sort things out. I should have stuck to trying to learn Chinese.

The cat is scratching at the door. I open the door and it circles my legs purring, the hypocrite. In those sapphire eyes I sense a know-it-all arrogance that reminds me of a guru I once met in my long ago search for truth. By the way I never found it, the truth I mean.

Cynthia falls asleep on the sofa, holding her cup of tea and mumbling nonsense. I silently put her cup on the coffee table. I am too tired myself to lead her to the bedroom. The phone rings somewhere in the apartment, I too must have fallen asleep on the sofa, because it is daylight. Cynthia is snoring. I step on something. It's Cynthia four front teeth. I was worried because her upper lip had caved in. Now I understand, poor Cynthia! Did she say she was married three or four times? I am not surprised, she really has gall. I search for what looks like a denture glass and I find it in the bathroom.

I should look after myself, I am stiff all over, and I have a kink in my neck from sleeping on the sofa. I need a long hot shower, a change of clothes, to snuggle back to bed refreshed with my daily crossword puzzle. It is too early to go back to my place and I don't even know who is squatting there either. I install Cynthia a bit more comfortably on the sofa, get a blanket for her and go explore what I can find in terms of toiletry. She is about my size so that part will be easy. There is a second bedroom, a guest bedroom, I suppose, with a bed that looks comfy enough. No books or crossword puzzles though. In the bathroom I find a bridge magazine; that will do. It will remind me of my childhood and my mother. Bridge magazines and politicians' declarations of intent are to me the most potent soporifics.

Cynthia shakes me awake. She is wrapped in a monogrammed bathrobe, bedecked with a frilly shower bonnet and wears exquisite kid leather mules.

"Come on, Clara Dear, we must go to your place." She is lisping so badly I can hardly make out what she is saying. I must have damaged her front teeth.

"You are not even dressed yet." I moan.

"I don't need to. I have the keys. Hurry up! Besides I have an appointment with the dentist in an hour, I have a terrible tooth-ache." she lisps with authority.

I have no idea what she is talking about, how did she get the keys to my place? Did she contact June or Harvey? I check my watch, it is eleven. I wrap myself in a blanket because after the shower I had snuggled naked into the bed. I feel like I could sleep another entire week without a break; so I am not going to ask too many questions. Adopt the path of least resistance. I get dressed in my dirty old clothes; I will change when I get home.

"I called the funeral parlor, it is all arranged. They will take care of everything. It will be a quiet service; Macky had given his instructions a while ago. He did not want anything fancy. The florist has been contacted and close friends have been informed. The celebration of life will take place next week at the Sheraton."

It strikes me like a thunderbolt. I am the widow! I am not sure I am up to playing this role. Yet, there is nothing I can change about it, what is done is done; I better hum along and try to remain gracious. My first widowhood was certainly not a picnic at the beginning; I don't suppose this one will be easy either, although riddled with different problems. I brace myself for unpleasant surprises.

Cynthia leads me to the apartment next door, Macky's place as I recall. Opens the door:

"This is your place now, Dear. We are truly neighbours. Welcome! I hope you will move in as soon as possible. From what Macky told me the place is all paid for." I am speechless. Rose garlanded wallpaper everywhere. Rich gaudy furniture with the tops covered with dainty doilies. The place smells of Macky's perfume, a trendy one I guess. I am getting a headache; my stomach is playing dirty tricks on me. How am I to break the news that I want a divorce?

"You will receive your marriage certificate and death certificate within the next 24 hours. In the meantime I think it is best for you to explore and get yourself accustomed to a new improved environment. You deserve every bit of it. I leave you to it, I must run to the dentist," lisps my companion.

She leaves the keys in the door and runs back to her affairs. I open wide the windows and rush to the bathroom. I need a moment or two to get adjusted. I am in a quandary, on one hand I would like to be kind to the memory of the poor fellow and on the other hand I am convinced I will not be able to assume the responsibility of such a heavy load. I need to get out of here. Since I don't know what to expect at my place and I am not ready for any more surprises I will go to have breakfast outside and then go to the library to sort my things out.

My mule cell phone rings. Without letting whoever is calling me talk, I shout:"Fuck off" and I turn the phone off. Macky's phone rings a few seconds later. I am not answering; there must be an answering device. After all I am a grieving widow. Yes, it is true that I grieve the poor gentle fellow who paid with his own life his understandable desire for a last kiss. When are we going to be able to stop that despicable practice of gay-bashing? There, sitting on his toilet, I cry over him and me and all of us. I am so tired and strung out emotionally, I wish I could die right there in the rose scented bathroom.

I search the drawers for a tissue to wipe my face. In the back of one I find a Ziploc bag filled with what I am sure is marijuana. I roll myself a joint like I have seen Edgar do it and I INHALE. Peace my friend! Now I have the giggles, I dance around Macky's apartment embracing my groom's ghost with one of his dainty doilies on my head as a bride's veil. I am off my rocker and it feels good. I better put some music on. The problem is, it is too far. My foot gets hooked on a Persian rug depicting what I take as an erotic scene. A kneeling George Bush is wooing Obama sprawled on a lounger wrapped in a doily and pink Eros sitting on a cloud grins happily; I fall flat on my face, my nose on Eros plump bum and I fall asleep.

A huge racket wakes me up, phones are ringing, someone is pounding at the door, I don't know why my head is under a coffee table that I don't recognize as mine. I feel as if I am dreaming a nightmare of noise. I better go to the door before they break in but I am in no mood to talk.

"At last!.. We were worried, I thought you took sick, Darling." Cynthia screams. "What in hell happened to you? When I left you, you were okay. Your hair is a mess." She embraces me "I should not have gone and left you alone in such dire circumstances. Don't fret, my Dear, I will be at your side." she rushes to answer the phone. I must be a sight. A fellow is behind her, I think it is the notary of last night. He shakes my hand: "I am one of the executors; Mrs. Weatherborne is the other one." he says with an encouraging smile. "I brought you the certificates we need to take care of the estate. I will do my utmost to expedite matters to your satisfaction. I recommend that you move into this apartment as soon as possible. You may retain your other domicile for a while if you so wish."

I am in total disarray, yet I react very poorly when I sense that one is trying to take charge of my affairs. It is true that I gave my consent to marry on his death bed a poor guy I hardly knew. A deal that was arranged by these two clowns hovering around me right now and I did not have the guts or the wits to walk out. I need time alone to recover my senses; meanwhile I am going to shut up and let them talk; I might get a better picture to plan my next move.

"You will need to explain to me very slowly what must be done because I am not swift when it comes to legalities," I tell Pink-tie. This is not true because I had to go through a lot of that same stuff when Edgar died. They did not ask for my resume and I am not going to provide them with one.

"This is not going to be difficult if you allow me to help you. You are the rightful heir of Mr. Fairmount's estate; I am one of the executors. We will go to the bank first so that you can have some funds right away to tide you over. Then, one step at a time, we will deal with all the other matters, such as the changeover of the ownership of the condo, the cars, the bonds etc. I will of course retain a certain amount for my services which is the normal procedures in a case like this. Rest assured that I will do my best to make things easier for you." This guy is a fancy talker alright. I am not sure I can trust him.

"Do you think I should consult a lawyer?" I ask.

"Remember that I am in the legal profession myself, so I don't think it necessary. I can take care of all the hurdles we encounter. However it is a choice you must make by yourself and if you decide you need a second opinion I can recommend some people I know."

During all this time, Cynthia, who is not lisping anymore has been exploring the apartment and filling big bags of stuff.

"I just got my things sorted out. Remember that I spent a few days tending Poor Dear Macky in this place. So I gathered what I brought over here, it's all in here." She shows me the bags. "Now the place is all yours, Darling Clara."

Why do I think I am being bamboozled?

"Now, if you don't mind I am going to my previous place, I have to meet somebody urgently." I say getting up. "I thank you very kindly for all the attention you have given me." I add for good measure.

"We must first go to the bank" Pink-tie says.

"That will have to wait until tomorrow or the day after" I say offhandedly.

"You need funds for all you have to do." Pink-tie argues.

"I'll manage," I retort. I leave after I made sure these two are out of my hair and I have secured both the keys and the certificates. I am going to sleep on that; yet in the back of my mind I think that I need an astute person to help me with this problem. I am considering having the marriage annulled. Is this possible when you are widowed?

There is a note from the superintendant taped on my door. It strikes me that with all the going-ons I am more than a week late for the rent. It is funny because it is the first time since I don't even remember when I have had so much cash at my disposal.

On the kitchen table there is a big bag of smoked salmon cut in cubes, Haida style, and a small vial of eulachon oil, with a note on it.

I am back at the hospital with Morgan, Harvey is gone. Where are you? Jeo wants you. Your nephew, Robin called 3 times. He says it's urgent. We are all worried. Please, call. Love. June.

I sit down overwhelmed, if I recall it is only a few weeks back that I was moaning for some entertainment, some exciting events to enhance my boring life. I now realize that too much entertainment can be just as boring. I am bored, bored, bored with all these demands for my attention. I cannot think straight anymore. Oh, my bed, my crossword puzzles, my evening music, I miss all that. Letting the world pass by, just waiting for the end twirling my thumbs. *"Get a grip, Clara!"* *"I will."*

Let's unravel the mess

In such a short while, I have become an aunt to Robin, a grand-mother to Jeo and Morgan, a substitute mother to June, a sister to Cynthia, and even a widow. Oops I almost forgot the mule business. I have lost the Clara I am comfortable with, devoid of crippling titles. I have been reacting to these assigned titles as I imagined I should, for outside that of widow, I never had to carry the burden of any of the other loaded roles. The only role I have been playing for the past fifteen years is that of the lonely, yet not lonesome, aging female senior slowly creeping towards oblivion. It is not a sad role nor is it idle as some thirty year old geriatric experts would tell you. It is a time of rearranging one's past to make a valid com-prehensible story of it even at the expense of hard facts. It is a time to face the truth of how stupid one was and must still be but don't know it. A time to contemplate benignly the utter folly of us humans. It is also a time to watch in the mirror in total amazement your skin fold a little bit more every day. A time to acquaint yourself with the body that you took for granted. Your failing organs demand it. Weak knees, slow digestion, blurred vision, sparser hair, delayed reactions, all that if you are like me in peak health for your age. That does not necessarily mean that one is barred from exploring new avenues, un-trodden paths but with very different perspectives. Caution should be the motto.

Am I ever in a philosophical mood! My recent widowhood must have triggered it. I am ready to unravel the mess I put myself in. First things first, I want to know what is happening to Jeo. I am going to go over to the hospital after I pay my rent. I hope an inspiration will come to me about how to deal with the two "executors". Maybe I am just paranoid, but better safe than sorry. I do not need Macky's money; I have survived decently enough with what I get. The end of the month pinch is not really a problem. What ticks me off is having anyone taking control of my life when I am not sure what motivates them.

Just as I am leaving, the phone rings. It is Robin.

"What ever happened to you? I tried to reach you all day yesterday. I am worried." he complains

"As much as I like you, Robin, don't expect me to give you an account of my whereabouts. If you want to know I have been busy with Jeo and his family and also with Macky. "

"I know of Jeo's recovery; June told me. That's super. I am all alone up here. I miss you. I also learned something that I'd rather tell you in person. You have a computer, maybe we could talk over Skype." he moans.

I don't have a webcam"

"Go get one, I'll pay for it."

"No need for it, it appears I have come into more money than I can deal with. I also have a lot to tell you. I cannot talk too long; I am on my way to the hospital to see Jeo. Toodleloo and all that sort of things." I hang up. As much as I love this tweety Robin I am in no rush to hear what he so desperately wants to tell me. I think it is not good news and I dread it. I have had my fill of bad news.

I still have the keys to Macky's car but I'd rather take the bus. It is not very safe to drive a dead man's car.

Jeo in a wheelchair is in the playroom of the ward enjoying himself in spite of his leg cast and various bandages. Someone seems to have forgotten the main reason he was placed in isolation, his contagious mumps. Bossy Morgan is there too, being Morgan, giving advice and organizing. I sit quietly and observe. Jeo's recovery is a huge load off my shoulders.

"Granny Clara, don't cry anymore I am going to take care of your boo-boo. Bob here is the nurse, he will give you nice medicine that won't hurt a bit." she says taking my presence for granted. Bob is a bald little boy who is obviously plagued with leukemia or a cancer of some kind. I don't think he is more than five years old. He smiles while pretending to prick me with a needle. I must not look sad.

"Granny Clara, what took you so long? I have been waiting for you all day!" Jeo who just noticed me exclaims and painfully rushes in his wheelchair to give me a one-armed hug. June walks in. As she sees me she grins happily. I feel welcomed, loved and needed. I am perking up.

"We are all going home tomorrow, Jeo has to stay another week to make sure that he is alright, but the doctor said, it is just standard procedure. We are so glad! Harvey left this morning with his father. Will you come and visit Jeo when we are gone?"

"Certainly! How are you faring yourself?"

"Not bad, still a bit weak, but so relieved to see Jeo up and about. Morgan is allowed to stay with me at the hospital for the night, so we won't be bothering you anymore. Everybody has been so kind! I don't know how to thank you. It is strange, we have known you such a short time and it feels as if you are family. We all do love you so much. We wish you would come and live with us and be our elder."

"I will visit for sure, and we can talk on the internet."

"It's not the same." she pouts.

"It will have to do, dear June, at least for the time being. I will be busy for a good month settling my affairs."

No more hasty commitments that I will regret. Although now that I might be able to afford a car, the idea of moving to Prince Rupert appeals to me a lot more but I want to have a few long sleeps before I make such a drastic decision. What if I get to the point that I cannot drive anymore for health reasons? I am not getting any younger and at my age I must consider this as an eminent possibility.

I leave the hospital light-hearted. I am going to unplug the phones, have a good rest, and then a stroll to my favourite spot along the seawall. I need to clear my head. It is a lovely day today, cool, breezy, invigorating; hopefully tomorrow will be the same.

It is ten at my clock radio, someone is pounding at my door and the cat who has been sleeping with me wants out. That cat does not want to get out of my life; I am due to have a serious talk with it. Cynthia erupts into my arms, kissing me, bad breath and all.

"Dear, dear Clara you left in a tizzy yesterday, I don't understand. Why are you so upset? I was so happy for you! Your buzzer did not answer, so I called lovely Marge your superintendant to let me in. I see you just got up, let me make you a nice cup of tea, we will talk." She is all business. I let her in and go to the bathroom to refresh myself but also to get my wits back in gear while she gets busy in the kitchen that smells of smoked salmon that I did not bother put in the fridge.

"Your phone is disconnected" she yells "what do I do to reconnect; I want to call Harry."

"Who is Harry?" I yell back sitting on the toilet in the Thinker's position.

"The notary, Dear."

"I don't want to see him, not yet. Please Cynthia give me a break." I lock the bathroom door and I turn the radio on. I always take my shower listening to the news so if it is bad news it goes down the drain. I hear Cynthia drag a chair to the bathroom door so she can converse with me in comfort. I get into the shower to drown out her voice. I let the water splash down my back, I take all my time carefully inspecting my toe nails and belly button but I cannot stay in there all day. As soon as I turn the water off, Cynthia resumes her coaxing. Why is she so keen? What is the ulterior motive? It can't be money; she is well-to-do by my books.

"I have great plans for the two of us now that you have come into money. Are we ever going to have fun!" she entices and adds: "after we properly mourn poor Macky of course!"

My ideas of fun surely do not jive with Cynthia's. I hesitate to break the news to her and I keep the door locked while I slowly oil my body with soothing cream. I brush my teeth one by one, checking if I still have a full set. Cynthia on the other side of the door keeps rambling about the fabulous times we could have together. I leave the water running so I am not listening. Then the sneaky witch starts sobbing loudly. I am a sap when I hear someone cry so I open the door.

"Where is that cup of tea you promised me?" I say now that I feel a lot more in control, wrapped in one of Edgar's old t-shirts smelling squeaky clean.

She jumps to attention with a grin on her face "Oh, dear, it must be cold by now. I'll make another one." she runs off to the kitchen giving me a few more minutes to compose myself as a strong determined opponent. I sit on my comfy chair, cross my legs and wiggle my bare toes.

Cynthia hands me the cup silently and sits down opposite me while I am searching for the right words for I do not want to hurt her delicate ego more than is necessary but I also do not want her to invade my privacy unduly. *"Easy, does it."*

"For the short while we have known each other, Cynthia, I have come to like and appreciate you a lot more than I thought I would when we met the first time."

"Oh! I love you Clara! We have become best friends; haven't we?"

"Cynthia, we do not know each other, I fear your world and mine are very different. I would hate for you to assume that I enjoy what makes you tick. That does not mean that we cannot be friends and see each other from time to time but I want to get things straight between us so you don't get any wrong ideas."

She frowns "You are telling me that we won't be friends anymore." She says with a quaver in her voice.

"Tell me, how long have you known Pink-tie, I mean the notary?"

"Oh, isn't he a Darling?"

"There you are doing it again! I hate it when you do that, the girlie-girl, the hair-brain, the higher-than-thou well connected woman of the world. All games! This is pure crap all these games you are playing. Especially when I know from experience that you are indeed a tough cookie. Don't get me wrong, I like your resilience. We are too old Cynthia to keep playing these idiotic games between the two of us. Do it with whomever you still can impress but not with me." I am pacing the floor between June's air mattress, the computer desk and the sofa. "Marge the sup's wife is not lovely Marge, she is a resentful mean hag, Pink-tie is not darling Harry, he is a conniving weasel; and you know it. I have seen you react in dangerous circumstances at the restaurant for example, after the shootings; you spotted the goon all by yourself on the cruising ship. You can be sharp, Cynthia, much more clever in many ways than I am. So please stop it and talk to me like the strong survivor that you are. Now I ask you again: when did you first meet Macky's notary? And whose idea was it that I marry ninety nine percent dead Macky? What's in it for you and for him?"

I have worked myself into a good snit. It is a fact that Cynthia aggravates me with all her pretending but I am mostly mad at myself for having said yes to their schemes. I don't need Macky's money, and I certainly could not live in his apartment with the cupids, the doilies and other paraphernalia of the male gay world. I don't want to be Cynthia's neighbour to have to hear reports of the latest news of the exclusive golf club she belongs to. Nor do I need reports on the Who-is-Who in town. How am I to get out of this predicament without hurting that nitwit of my so-called friend?

Cynthia has shrivelled to a dejected lump in her armchair. I sit on the floor at her feet. Anyone would have said to me half of what I just said to her I would have scrammed never to see that person again. That's how crazy proud I am. I admire in people the grits to take blows and keep at it.

"Talk to me about yourself, your true self. I don't want to hear of all the marvellous people you happen to know; I want to hear about you. You don't need to try to impress me. I am already impressed. You have already proven to me that you are gutsy; you can also be kind and considerate. This is what I like about you. " I coax.

"There is not much to say."

"You mentioned in the hospital that you have been married four times. There has to be a story to that. Who was your first husband?"

She snickers. "My first husband was my father's best friend. He was fifty one when I married him; I was eighteen. I was his third wife. He dressed me, sent me to etiquette classes, and showed me around like a trophy. He treated me like a stern parent and I obeyed him. He was polishing on what my father had fashioned me to be. He impressed me with all his savvy. We had all the material things we needed and then some."

"How did you get along sexually with you so young and him on the downhill slope?"

"Sexually?" she repeats as if she never heard the word before. "I don't know; we got along, I guess."

"What happened to him? Did you divorce?"

"No; he died five years after we married, a heart attack. By the time I was twenty three I was a widow. I went back to live with my parents, my father was managing my affairs. He also found me a second husband but this one was not very trustworthy according to my father and he convinced me to get a divorce. I felt relieved at the time because I did not care much for that one. He did not have proper personal hygiene and always smelled unpleasantly."

"How old were you by then?"

"Twenty eight."

"What did you do after the divorce?"

"I went on a cruise with my parents. My father had just retired. We went all the way to Rio. That was fun and on the ship I met the most handsome man. He was travelling with his mother. We befriended them, it was lovely. I think I was in love for the first time in my life. My father did all the inquiries about the family and a year later we were married. It was that day at the hotel in the wedding suite that he told me he was gay. For the sake of our parents we decided we would stay together and make as if. Although I was pretty sad at first, I must admit that it is also the day I gained some more freedom. If there is something Jeffrey taught me, it was not to tell my parents everything I did or thought. We were 'happily' married for ten good years. "

"Did he die too?"

"No, Jeffrey is well, I see him once in a while, when he happens to be in Canada. He lives in Mexico with his partner. We are friends of sorts. After both our mothers passed away, my father was in poor health. He wanted me to come back and live with him. Jeffrey had finally the freedom to live his life the way he chose which meant without me around and especially not my father whom he hated with a passion. So we divorced."

"And you went back to live with your father? What about the fourth guy?" I can see that this woman paid a huge price for her financial and social comfort under the thumb of her monstrously selfish father. I mentally thank my parents for their aloofness in regards to my well-being. Yet I can see that we are both products of upper middle class post-colonialist parents. The not necessarily religious but regular church attendants, the staunch supporters of residential schools for Indian children, the founders of exclusive golf clubs banned to Jews and coloured people, the pillars of the New Frontier society. I suppose it is what happened in every part of North America.

And now I am back on my righteous podium, I forgot Cynthia, the lonesome woman and her desperate attempt to connect with me, the callous one. Let's forget the fourth husband, it is, I am sure, another catastrophe.

"So, Cynthia, do you have any more prospects in sight, marriage wise?"

"Oh, dear, no! It was my father, rest his soul, who always wanted me properly looked after," she exclaims. When she utters the word FATHER, there is an unmistakable reverence in her voice. I can hear that the fellow had totally hypnotized her from the cradle on, she is in awe after years of submission and she will not shake it off.

"I still don't understand why it seems so important for you that we remain friends."

"I don't know. I feel so lonely sometime. It is not that I am not busy. I go to a lot of functions, I attend events, I know a lot of people but nobody is close to me. With you I feel a connection. We have fun together and I can cry or laugh. You don't judge me." That is where she is wrong. I do judge and too many times not in her favour.

"I am not lonely, but I am a loner. I am very jealous of my space. I get by on a small budget although it is true that I find it a bit restrictive at times. I don't know why I gave in to marry Macky on his deathbed. I must have been very tired after what happened to Jeo and poor Macky. Now I am in a position where it seems that people I never met before are taking over and are trying to reorganize my life. I find that unbearable.

"How well do you know the notary? I am not sure I can trust him. You see, I made a mistake, what is done is done, but I want to be extremely careful as to how I will proceed."

"All I know is that this notary has been Macky's legal advisor for some time. He is the new partner of Macky's ex."

"Why would he care so much if Macky's estate goes to me a perfect stranger rather than the government?"

"I don't know but you have a point. It all started when Macky's ex came for a visit at the hospital, I don't know what was said between the two, I did not stay in the room. After the visit, Macky was very upset and told me he wanted to change his will that was still set in favour of his ex. He gave me his notary's office number. When I called he was not in his office and since it was an emergency the secretary gave me her boss's home number. It was Macky's ex's number. I added it all up but I did not say anything. Then Macky wanted to leave his estate to a non-profit organization dealing with bullying and gay-bashing and for me to have his car. I don't drive and I told him so. I use taxis. So I suggested that he leave the car to you because I could see that you really enjoyed it. Your face lit up when Macky offered you the car to go to your cabin a few weeks back." Cynthia is getting more animated. She holds my hands.

"Yes. So what happened next?"

"After you told me that you did not want the car and explained why, the notary became very interested in you. He asked all sorts of questions."

"Did you tell him I was a pauper and a dumb old broad?"

Cynthia is upset. "I would never say anything like that. No I said that I had not known you for a long time but I appreciated you as a great person, resourceful and kind. Macky also said that he liked you. Then the notary suggested the marriage. Macky thought about it and agreed that it was a good idea. He even made a joke saying that on his deathbed he would finally comply with his parents' wishes. The rest you know."

"Thank you Cynthia, I hope you will understand that now I need to be alone for a good twenty four hours. I will keep you in the loop."

She kisses me warmly and leaves full of dignity. I appreciate her tactfulness. I prepare for a long walk along the seawall. It seems like ages that I haven't done just that; it might inspire me.

That walk feels refreshing, not too many people on the path, a blue sky, light breeze. It clears my head because I deliberately opt not to dwell on my problems; just counting the cargo ships entering or leaving the harbour, admiring the foliage in the process of changing colors, feeling my muscles slowly regaining their elasticity and silently thanking Mother Earth for allowing me to witness all that. I am content in my four dimensions.

As I turn the key at the main door of my apartment building, a name comes to my mind: Tony. Wily Tony the fox! I am sure he knows lawyers, good ones. I will call him but I must first find his number. I am positive I did not throw away the paper where Harvey jotted down the number back in Prince Rupert. That's when he offered me, in a round about way, to be a mule for his organization. I will search all my pockets. All of a sudden I am so excited, I can hardly breathe. The cat of course is with me; we rode the elevator together. If that cat thinks I am going to marry it too I have news for it; even if it has become my regular bed pal, a kind of consort on the sly. Never mind how handsome it is, that beast is bad news all over for me, and that's a reality.

I find the lawyer's letter that I was supposed to destroy; I forgot to comply. I find the envelope, Hair-do Jennifer handed me in the taxi, I forgot to open it. I have Harvey's Paradise business card, a fancy drawing by Jeo; I am not too sure what it represents. I retrieve all kinds of information about abortions I had printed out at the library back in Prince Rupert. I am getting frustrated. I stop, make myself a cup of tea and finish the box of cookies I had bought for June and Morgan. My place is in shambles so the best thing is to tidy up. I start by deflating the air mattress. I use the reverse electric pump for the job, patting myself on the back for having bought it. While the pump is doing its job I clean the milk stains on the carpet and put the smoked salmon in small zip lock bags in the fridge. Then I go to my computer to check my emails. Five from Robin. I will answer later. Now that the air is completely sucked out I fold the air mattress, right under it is my airplane ticket, still in my cleaning frenzy I pick it up to throw it in the garbage; that's where I find the paper I was looking for, folded in the ticket. Huge relief! I sit and think. I have to figure out exactly what I want from Tony the sleaze. All these activities put me to sleep right on the sofa – I am getting old.

I wake up in a panic -- what if it is too late to call Tony? It's only nine thirty so I'll try my luck. After two rings I hear his distinctive voice, nonchalant yet alert.

"Yes, can I help you?"

"Tony, maybe you remember me, it's Clara. I need some expert legal advice as soon as possible."

"How soon is soon?"

"By tomorrow at the latest."

"Call your lawyer, not me."

"That's just it, I don't know any sharp lawyer."

"Ha! That kind of lawyer! What happened to you Clara, I thought you were cleverer than putting yourself in a mess."

"It is not what you think Tony. It is trickier than that and not illegal if that is what you have in mind."

"I am on my way to a restaurant to meet a friend. I am intrigued. Can meet for a few minutes at the bar at Casa di Antonio?"

I get a jolt, the very same place where the shooting occurred.

"I would rather not, that place is not very healthy for me." No one is going to make me set foot in that restaurant anymore, no matter what the circumstances are. Yet it is interesting that Tony would be a client. It takes a little while but eventually Tony agrees to pick me up and talk in his car on the way to the restaurant then I will be on my own to return home. That suits me fine because the very idea of setting foot in there puts me in a panic. In the car I explain the hasty marriage and how suspicious I am of Pink-tie. "I smell a rat," he says and which might prove he has read his classics or at least finished grade nine in a regular class.

As I leave Tony's car in front of the ill-omened dive, Tony has assured me that I would receive a call tomorrow morning from someone he knows and that someone will stay at my side during my dealings with Pink-tie. He says that when the notary sees this lawyer he will not need further explaining to tow the line.

I get back home hugely relieved. I know Tony will be true to his word. I actually might end up my late senior years as a well-to-do lady.

Soaring in the thereafter

 T wo months have gone by. It has been an exceedingly busy time for me. I have not made much effort to be in the Now nor have I dwelt much in the Then. My attention has been constantly challenged by these new adventures so strange to me. Macky's life has been celebrated with dignity; the gay community was well represented. I had a few eye to eye discussions with the cat that I have now accepted to call Winston although I am not sure it makes much difference to it. I think the egos of cats are way beyond humane preoccupations such as names. Cynthia was true to her words in helping to rearrange Macky's apartment more to my liking; I kept one doily for memory's sake and moved to his place. I have driven Cynthia back and forth to some of the endless functions she delights in attending. So far I have refused to go further than the door to these kudos distributing events. Jeo is back home doing well. June perked up; I have conversations with the family every other day on Skype. I have to admit that my involvement with the young family is getting deeper and certainly brings richness to my life. Robin is coming to town next week; he will stay at my place for the weekend; I am trying to convince him to return to university to finish his studies. Meanwhile he promised to teach me how to smoke bubble hash. It is apparently tricky. I have also decided that to be a mule is not my cup of tea; Tony has been most gracious about it. I now have the means to take the whole family to the Seattle zoo for Christmas. I will have to make sure I have a will and I also know who is sure to have their education financially secured. It might take some tweaking but I am getting good at it. Tony's lawyer has been a mentor of sorts. He was well worth the investment. Harvey's father, the shaman, is dining with me as soon as he has finished his round of proselytizing. Next month I am starting paragliding lessons. I have tried it twice now in tandem with a pro; I found the experience exhilarating. I am trying slowly to adjust a fitting routine to my life, resuming my walks along the seawall and my weekly visits to the library although I have not found much time to read to my heart's content.

I have tea with Cynthia every other day but I am soon going to space it to once a week and possibly only twice a month. I have introduced an activity that is immensely rewarding and helps me keep an even keel to what I consider a hectic life. I take Macky's car, drive a few miles along the sea to sky highway screaming and singing to my heart's needs along the way. I always come back from those expeditions refreshed and ready to face the challenges of this newly acquired social life that built itself around my monkish tendencies. It will soon be Christmas; Cynthia wants to celebrate in style. She is planning a big reunion that we two are supposed to host; I am not sure it is a good idea. I have already cut down on half of the bashes she has been scheduling. Reunions of the sort make me very nervous; I'd rather listen to the rain beating my windows, cuddled in my favourite armchair with a good book than passing the turkey dish around. Affluence has lots of draw-backs! I remember my mother entertaining my father's cohorts of well appointed, full of themselves tipsy monkeys. No wonder she felt compelled to hit the sauce too. How else can you bear the small talks, innuendos and wheeling-dealings for hours on end? PEACE ON EARTH! Jollies give me the creeps.

Harvey's father called this morning; Merle is his name. He will be in town tomorrow and asked if he can drop by. I am delighted; he is just the man I wanted to see. Cynthia must attend another of her fundraising galas for the benefit of some obscure charitable organization therefore will be out of my way. She has been busy shopping for the proper garb undergoing anxiety attacks over choices of colour and style. She is also determined to recruit me onto the board of directors of her favourite not-for-profit society. I don't think I am cut out for it; I prefer to contribute in a more personalized fashion and retain control as to where my money goes. Some of the charitable organizations have outrageous administration fees and the money goes mostly to pay the fat salaries of professional fundraisers and CEOs rather than to whom or what it is intended.

I am seriously thinking about selling this apartment and moving to a trailer park where Cynthia would be reluctant to visit me. What holds me back is that, as a rule, trailer parks are more in the vicinity of liquor stores than libraries. Trailer parks also are not known to be great on privacy. I still like the woman but although she tries very hard to accommodate my need for solitude I find her to be on the heavy side maintenance wise. Nothing is perfect.

Romantic interlude

Today is the tomorrow I expected. Merle should arrive soon. He has phoned me several times since I first met him at the hospital for Jeo. He claims we share a link and although I am not sure what he means I indeed sense a link deep inside me. I like to hear him talk, he seems anchored and humble about it unlike many gurus I have met in the past. The knowledge of the West Coast First Nations fascinates me and I find their expression in art awesome but I am particularly interested in their views on death.

In street clothes, thrift store style, my style too, I would not have recognized Merle. The only time I saw him was at the hospital and he was dressed in full regalia wrapped in a magnificent button blanket. He is an average size man, long jet black hair tied in a pony tail. He looks very shy. We shake hands formally. This might not be easy since I am shy too and still not at home in Macky's apartment. I offer him some refreshments. He opts for tea and follows me to the kitchen where he sits at the counter. I had in mind to entertain him in the living room but the kitchen is good too. Macky's kitchen is full of gadgets for which I have no use and I have difficulty finding the simplest things. Cynthia is more adept than me at tea ceremonies. There is a teapot somewhere and a full set of dainty Royal Dolton tea cups but I dump two teabags in the pot of boiling water and pull out my own mugs from the only cupboard I have explored so far. As I am preparing tea, Merle scans the kitchen with a puzzled look on his face.

"This place does not look like you at all. I am surprised; I had imagined different surroundings for you."

I laugh so hard I almost spill the boiling hot tea on Merle's lap. I sit down and wipe my eyes. That laugh is so liberating; it is the first I have been able to bring out of myself in the last two months.

"Oh, Merle you are so perceptive. I have desperately tried to feel at ease in this apartment. I have tried to be nice, accommodating, not hurt other people and I was wondering what was really wrong with me for this is much better in terms of space, furnishings or commodities and whatnots than the other place I was living in, yet I don't feel right in it; it seems to rub me against the grain."

"I know what you mean; I have felt this several times in my life. Once I remember I was offered a good paying job in the city, it was supposed to be my chance to be a responsible taxpaying citizen in my country watching and counting carefully the loading and unloading of cargo ships off the harbour. A nice meaning person found the job for me. That was with the rightful intention to 'rehabilitate me'. I tried very hard to comply; I arrived on time, sober, full of good will. Yet I felt miserable. The terrible urge to drink myself into oblivion was so strong that I almost gave in to it. Instead I quit the job and I am afraid I let down the good soul who had sponsored me." He shrugs. "Oh, well, try to do good to a rabid dog and it will bite you." And he laughs.

We are facing each other sitting on real leather upholstered high stools at the kitchen counter that forms an island in the middle of the room; above us hanging from the ceiling there is a fair size wooden rack and on the rack hang various shining copper pots and skillets. This is a serious kitchen for up-to-date informed yuppies who can concoct a dish of linguini alfredo in a jiffy. We remain quiet, sipping tea. It is a nice blank moment. I don't know if we are in the Now, the Then or the After and it does not matter.

Merle starts humming softly, gently rocking his body from left to right.

"Wait I know that song! It's 'No regrets', the French Edith Piaf used to sing it."

He puts his arm around my shoulders, I reciprocate, and thus arm in arm and rocking we belt out:

No! No regrets
No! I will have no regrets
All the things
That went wrong
For at last I have learned to be wise

We slowly get up and dance smiling at each other, we miss a word or two filling in with whatever comes to mind, la la la la la la.

No! No regrets
No! I will have no regrets
For the grief la la
la la la
I've forgotten the past

And the memories I had
I no longer desire
Both the good and the bad
I have flung in a fire
la la la (bis) (bis) (again and again)

No! No regrets
No! I will have no regrets
All the things that went wrong
For at last I have learned to be wise

there we wink at each other.

> *No! No regrets*
> *No! I will have no regrets*
> *For the seed that is new*
> *It's the love that is growing for you*

We belt the last words to the top of our voice enlaced we kiss the sweetest of kisses. The phone rings. I let the answering machine do its job. Unfortunately or fortunately it's on loudspeaker. Robin's voice booms across the apartment.

"Hello Auntie, I will be at your place in less than an hour. I hope you have coffee ready, I will supply the donuts. Lot's to tell you; brace yourself." He hangs up before I can reach the phone.

I look at Merle, Merle looks at me. The phone rings again. The answering machine broadcasts Cynthia's voice: "Hello, my darling Clara, I got off early - boring convention - don't bother picking me up I will get a taxi and get some blueberry tarts on the way to your place. Please make some tea. Monkish you! When are you going to learn to be sociable and pick up the phone when it rings?"

Merle looks at me, I look at him. "Let's get out of here fast!" he says putting his coat back on. "Are you coming?" I am coming. Once again I find myself in the stairwell of this building descending the fifteen flights of stairs to avoid meeting my well-wishers. Except this time I do it giggling all the way with someone holding my hand tight.

"Where do you want to go?" he asks.

"Nowhere in particular, let's walk."

"You don't mind the rain?"

I had not noticed that it was raining. In winter in Vancouver you only notice when it is sunny. If you don't like rain, move to Arizona, which is where many affluent seniors from here spend the winter months. I like the rain like some people back east like snow.

"Our ancestors used to go naked in the rain, not to wet their clothing. I still do it sometime when I am at the reserve just to get the feel of it. Have you ever been in the buff outside on a rainy day? It's an empowering experience."

"I would not go so far, my body is used to wearing clothes but I enjoy the feeling of rain on my face. I like the gray sky looming so low over me. I also like taking shelter under a big tree; I like the different resonance of the traffic when the streets are wet."

"The instant I saw you enter Jeo's room in the hospital, I knew I had to get in touch with you. I want to know all about you and I want you to know all about me. There was power in that room and you were instrumental in it almost more than I was. Tell me why it is that you live in such a foreign place?"

We walk and I talk; starting with the meeting of the cat up to now. We stop for a coffee and a sandwich and we walk and talk some more. He tells me that I should not use the word shaman for what he is doing; that shaman is a foreign word. He says that he is still learning to be a proper medicine man. It is a long process in the best of cases but nowadays it is even more difficult for there are so few elders to show the way and so much need. He tells me that his people are still on the path of recovery. It is a long arduous unknown road.

We are back in front of my building. We are dripping wet and smiling. Robin calls me from his car. He steps out and runs to me, arms out for a hug. The two men size each other up.

"I knew you must have gone walking, so I waited." he beams.

"Shall we all go upstairs, I need to change and I would not mind a cup of hot cocoa. What about it you guys?"

"Right on, I have donuts."

"I think Cynthia has some goodies too, if she did not eat them all waiting for me. Then we can have a party."

I must admit that in spite of my elated mood the party is not going too well. Each one claims me as their best friend and regards the other as intruder. Cynthia is the most polite of them. She has some savvy yet she expects Robin and Merle to leave before she does. When I tell her that I have invited both of them to stay over-night she seems most surprised and a bit disappointed.

"Well it is your place MyDear, and you do with it as you see fit," she says with a pinched face and leaves with the protesting cat in her arms.

I had no idea that she saw herself as my benefactor of sorts, having pulled me out of my squalor to elevate me to a much improved way of life. Outside of all her qualities she is a needy person. It is also my error to have been compliant to her for the past two months. She must have taken my confused state as Macky's widow for lack of character. Maybe she has come to think I owe her or worse that she owns me like she does the cat. I have got sad news for her, poor Cynthia.

It is true that the past eight weeks have been a hectic time for me for which I was totally unprepared. I give myself a pat on the back though for my insight about the pink-tied notary executor. The lawyer took care of it; there was some timid embezzlement, it seemed that was settled out of court. I was however relieved that Cynthia was absolutely cleared as far as money was concerned. The lawyer also assured me that I am now a well-to-do lady and appointed, for my convenience, a financial counselor whom I can consult should I plan on any large expenses. This is something I appreciate since I consider myself a drooling idiot in money matters. I still have to draft a will now that the cat provided me with a family. It would be nice to secure at least Joe, Morgan and Robin's educa-tion and give them the tools to become whatever they are born to be. To struggle to secure your next sandwich is a counterproductive and debilitating experience.

No, my unease, my funky mood, comes from that place in which I now live. I don't seem to be able to fit in it. I let Cynthia's projec-tions of my needs take over, while I was busy dealing with bankers and other officials. It is not my place; it is a Macky-Cynthia place. I feel as if my privacy is being violated. Cynthia's frantic activi-ties create a whirl wind around me. I can no longer spend the day just looking at the ceiling, dreaming when I get the urge. I cannot anymore read a fascinating book very late into the night because I know that she is going to knock at my door at nine in the morning all dolled up to invite me to join her for breakfast at some blasted fundraising event. We are supposed to meet Elgenor Simpson-Black who made his money in the mining business, the clever fellow, and sponsors the hard of hearing. His mother died deaf when she was ninety eight, and that is still moving him to tears. When you have a heart...

When I go for a walk, she joins me. She even got herself a super trendy jogging suit, and chats all the while; when I tell her to shut up, she cries and her dentures make funny clicking noises in her mouth. I tried to give her some of Macky's stash of pot to inhale but she says she has had poor lungs since she contracted pneumonia when she was eight. She prefers the white powder. That might explain why she is always so geared up.

With Cynthia's grand departure there has been a lull in the conversation, my two men are subdued. I get up and announce that I will prepare the spare bedroom for Robin. Robin follows me somehow eager to be alone with me; he closes the door and sits on the bed, this is the first time I have seen him since Prince Rupert and of course this is the first time also that he is at my new address, he whistles:

"Classy digs!" he exclaims sotto voce.

"Well, you are welcome to it if you so wish."

"Nice location too. The mule business must be paying well. I am not sure about the furnishings nor the decorations though. It is not you as I pictured it."

I have kept Robin in the dark about my recent widowhood. Somewhere in the back of my mind I have not made peace with it. I am also a bit ashamed of it even though I gave, in Macky's name, a fair amount of money to a philanthropic society bent on educating teens on the acceptance of gay kids.

"By the way, who is this guy loitering in your living room?" he inquires suspiciously.

"You mean, Merle? He is my lover."

I see the shock on his face. As a matter of fact he looks postively disgusted. Young people have many preconceived ideas about old people. I cannot blame him; I would have reacted exactly the same way at his age. Romance, in certain circumstances, might still be admissible but sex is perfectly ridiculous.

I sit beside him on the bed and try to put my arm on his shoulder. He pulls away.

"How long have you been dating him?" he asks.

"It's our first date, don't ruin it, please. It could just be a fling but I want to be able to enjoy it to the fullest for the time it lasts." I beg. "I have a lot to tell you and some of it is good news for a change."

"And I have some news also, that I have been trying to tell you for a while and you keep putting me off. I don't understand why. This is one of the reasons I am here today. I thought we were going to spend some time together, just the two of us. Instead I have to attend some sort of convention with foolish Cynthia and that dude. Auntie Clara, you have changed and not for the better." he moans.

"Look, you must be tired after the long drive, why don't you sleep on it and tomorrow I promise the day is just for you and me. I can't wait to hear all that you have to say, I have so much to tell you too! I am so very glad to see you. Please give me one of these big hugs that you are so good at." I think I got him to relax. It is not easy to be a parent. "There are two bathrooms in this place; yours is just next to your room. Good night sweet Robin!"

He hugs me reluctantly. "Good night to you too!" Did I detect a touch of sarcasm? I'll let it go at that and leave closing the door.

Merle is reading in the living room; he lifts his head above the newspaper: "Who is this guy to you?" he says with a frown.

"Robin is my late husband's son. It is a long story and I don't want to talk about it right now. Do you want to stay for the night?"

"I thought you would never ask." He takes my arm "You lead the way I have until seven tomorrow morning. My plane leaves at nine."

How sweet it is to share a bed; I had almost forgotten. We hug, we giggle, we snuggle, and we cuddle under the forgiving downy quilt. It is fun, tender, uplifting. I didn't think I had it in me anymore. It is the first time since Edgar died. My wrinkled skin caressing and being caressed shoots delicious waves of pleasure to the core of my body. I am loving me and thus the entire world. I am embracing life. That beats meditation or searching for clues in Wikipedia. It also beats Thomas Haas blueberry tarts that supposedly send Cynthia to Nirvana.

We wake up at six, we kiss again and I make coffee. I leave a note for Robin who is still asleep and we drive to the airport. We hardly talk, there is nothing to say and it is good not to have to entertain, to be at ease without the need of chatting about innuendos. We part with a wink, good friends.

"Drop by whenever you can." I say with a smile.

"Will do." he replies. I know he will. We refrain from kissing to not shock possible onlookers.

"Murder!" He says

Robin is up sulking over a cup of coffee. I hug him: "I am happy, you are here with me at last!" I say encouragingly sitting down across from him.

"The dude is gone?"

"The dude's name is Merle, I like him." I rebut. He grunts.

"Now I am going to tell you everything that happened since Prince Rupert. It has been two grueling months for me and for you too, I imagine. Let's get reacquainted. Have breakfast and let me talk." I am ready to take the lead.

Robin knew of Macky's accident and I had told him when he died, but what I had omitted was my wedding, probably because I am uncomfortable with it. So now he knows.

"That's disgusting! How could you do such a thing?" He sounds totally dismayed.

Youth, always ready to flaunt their clean ideals of a perfect post-card world.

I explain the circumstances, the very little time I was given to make a well-thought out decision, the former partner and his not so clean notary of a lover. I mention that I have not spent a cent of the money I inherited; that outside of the apartment I have a really hard time making my own I still live on almost the same budget.

He sits there in a slump, in front of his cup of coffee, elbows on the table covering his face with his hands. I must change tack. I don't want to lose him for Edgar's sake and my sake too for I have come to love him.

"The one thing I am happy about is that now I have the means to send you back to college where you belong and stop you on your track to hoodlumry. It is something that your Uncle Ed could not do."

"It is too late anyway." He says with a fatalistic shrug.

"What do you mean?"

I came here to tell you that I am on my way to do Tony in with his own gun, the bastard." He gets up.

"Hold your horses, young man. Are you out of your mind? Don't you think I ought to know what prompts you to do such a stupid thing? I am the rightful widow of your Uncle Ed, don't forget."

"I have been trying to tell you for some time, you won't listen. You keep putting me off. Tony the slum bag is the one who put a contract out on Uncle Ed. I now know that for a fact."

It is my turn to sit.

"I want you to start from the beginning. How can you be so sure?" I choke out.

It is a fact that when I found Edgar dead in our car I was in shock; nothing that day prepared me for it. He had been in the best of moods for a change that very day and he had left just for a car wash. When he did not return and I had to leave to go to work, I thought he had stopped for a friendly conversation with someone in the building. He knew I needed the car. So I went directly to the garage. That is where I found him, slumped over the dash board, still holding the gun and with that tiny hole in his head. I hollered; someone called 911. The police came. There was an investigation, I was questioned endlessly. Two months later the police concluded it was a suicide.

I was left devastated, sad and resentful all at once but also financially strapped with all the debts I did not even know he had incurred in our name. To my dismay the credit cards were maxed out; I did not have time to sit down and suspect foul play and to tell the truth I did not want to think about it. It scared me. Several years later, when doubt would creep in on my mind I willfully opted for the police version, suicide. I never found the courage to delve into Edgar's shady activities that were mentioned so often during the investigation.

Now I have to stop Robin from doing the monstrously idiotic thing that he is so ill-prepared to accomplish. Robin the romantic fool! The rightful son of his father! The comic book hero!

On the unconditional path of revenge, sullen Robin is not looking at me. Standing feet wide apart, hands in his pockets, he seems determined to challenge me and the world. I must find the right words fast. This unexpected late parenthood has me baffled.

"If you tell me how you came to the conclusion that Tony is responsible for your father's death, I will tell you all I know. Then we can compare notes. If you convince me, I will help you bury Tony in a cement slab," I promise viciously.

He sits down again and places the gun on the table. That's good. I gained a bit of time in a potentially explosive situation. I should not hail victory though; his eyes are cast down, and he is very agitated.

"The day after you left me alone up there, a fellow showed up at the cabin, I came out to greet him – I felt very lonely – but the guy stopped right in his tracks and told me not to come closer. He looked very scared. I thought he was high on something so I stayed put. He asked me my name. I told him; that seemed to reassure him and he followed me inside. He had come to pick up the merchandise I had prepared. It was late so I offered for him to crash at the cabin before turning back. He said he had gotten himself a room at a motel nearby."

This is going to take time; I go and brew some more coffee. There is a state of the art espresso machine in Macky's kitchen but I still don't know how to operate it and Cynthia only drinks tea so she can't help me. I have my own percolator, it is not cool but it does the job.

"Keep talking, I am listening."

"You remember I had paid for your room at Harvey's motel. Since you were gone, I thought I might as well use the commodities. It is not the greatest but you can have a decent shower and I felt closer to you. So, once I had finished what I had to do, I went to spend the night down there. That's where the guy was staying too. He was into the sauce already when I arrived and in a talkative mood. We got into talking and he told me I gave him the creeps because I looked so much like someone he had helped to bump off right when he was starting on the job. He said he had been the lookout for the job; he was just a kid then. He said the guy he was working with was a real psycho but a 'clean' worker and they heard later that it had been ruled as a suicide."

"That's not enough information. Did you ask for a name?"

"He said he was not sure anymore but it was something Italian like Vitrolo. A loser he added"

"A loser? Aren't we all? Listen, whether we get to Tony today or tomorrow does not matter really after all this time; let's go for a last walk you and I."

"A last walk? What do you mean?"

"Well, if you think that Tony is going to go down easy I have news for you or if you think we are clever enough to do it without being caught you must be dreaming. So either we die or we go to jail for a very long time. If your mother can still see you she is going to be totally devastated. After all she tried to raise you so that you would have a happier life than she had and that you would be sturdier than your biological father."

I let that sink in for a while. That was clever of me to bring Robin's mother into the picture. He told me he loved her. I give myself a pat on the back and keep busy in the kitchen before I drop my other argument.

"It is really too bad because I had in mind to help you go back to your studies in botany. You could have lived here with me for a while until you are back on your feet I am also now in a position to supply food and tuition." I say all that casually while getting dressed to go out.

He gets up and puts the gun in his pocket.

"Unless you plan on shooting seagulls, I don't think we will need it because Tony with his gorgeous Italian shoes is not going to be found on a muddy path." Finally Robin smiles.

"This is why I need you so much Auntie Clara; you are so wise and so funny. I don't want you to get involved; I am going to do this by myself."

Did I sense a small faltering of resolve in his tone of voice or is it just wishful thinking?

"Let's not talk about that for a while and enjoy this lovely day. There is a task for you; you will teach me the name of each bloom that we can spot in the dead of winter. Please don't tell me the Latin names I will never be able to remember. My poor doting brain is not meant for this kind of information I much prefer the English words, they can be so romantic – Dandelions, Morning Glories, Buttercups…"

We are out on a sunny day for a change. Robin is mulling over his options I gather; I won't disturb him. Meanwhile I am wondering if I should get in touch with Tony. I think I could convince him to let go of Robin, if I pay back what he has invested in the young man and promise absolute discretion from both of us. Edgar is dead, there is nothing I can do about it; he will be alive in my memory as long as I live but I must save his son from a fate not much different from his father's. It would be too outrageously stupid.

If it is true that Tony put a contract out on Edgar he will owe me and I think he knows it, otherwise why would he have sent me that money? Why would he try to recruit me as a dumb mule? A job, he knows, I am hardly cut out to perform! Why would he have been so eager to accept my resignation? Why would he have helped me recruit a mighty astute lawyer to solve Macky's estate conundrum? It might be because he is trying to redeem himself. Well in that case I will try to help him a little further in his redemption, but first I must placate Robin for a while to get time to do my own investigation.

On the way back, I propose to drive to the university campus.

"You could try to catch one of your former teachers, or some friends. It must be a while since you have haunted the campus. I could drop you off and pick you up in a few hours. Just for old time's sake."

"Are you serious about being able to foot the tuition fees? I could work part time at some dumb job to help."

"I told you I am in a position to support you. That would be for me an honourable way to spend the money I inherited. Remember Robin, you are a little bit the son I never had and Edgar, wherever he is, would be a lot happier to know that you are safe. He was a gentle fellow and totally against violence."

"That is true; he told me once that violence was for the weak at heart; that I should use my noodle."

"If only he could have practiced a little more what he was preaching and use his noodles as he called it, you and I would not be in such a mess!"

I think I am slowly inching through to Robin's thick skull. His murderous determination is weakening by the minute. Lucky for me because I am getting cold outside and I long for a nice luxurious hot bath alone; hopefully Cynthia will be gone to one of her fundraising luncheons. I also need time by myself to call Tony.

I am lounging on my bed, wrapped in my comfy robe; Robin calls in the best of mood, he says that he will be getting a ride back and will stop to buy some food because he noticed my fridge was empty. Supper is on him. Cynthia also called to say she will be staying for supper at a dear old friend. It is time to try to reach Tony.

He answers from his cell, he is in the neighborhood and will stop by my place; he is curious to see my new environment. His lawyer friend told him it was interesting. He should have seen it before I moved in.

Tony the contractor, or not?

"Hello there old girl; I see you are living it up! Marrying an old fag on his deathbed. Aren't you ashamed?"

"As a matter of fact, yes, I am ashamed if you want to know, and if I could reverse the decision I would. But as it is I have got to live with it as best I can."

"Shame is a waste of time, darling Clara, just as much as pride. Acknowledge your mistakes and learn from them if you can. But you did not call me to confess your sins, you sneaky little vixen. By the way how is your protégé?"

"To whom are you referring to; may I ask?"

"I am talking about our Robin, my dear. He is in town I heard."

"You seem to know a lot of things. But I am glad you mention him because that is the exact reason I called you. What I want to know is what it would take for you to accept his resignation."

"I am not ready for that. He is a good clean worker. Believe me they are hard to find. He is a clever young fellow too and knows his stuff."

"He told me he owes you a lot of money. I would be ready to pay back all he owes you with interest if you want. He is not a squealer. You can be sure of that," I offer stealthily.

"Clara, Clara, stop beating around the bush. What are you scared of and what do you want from me this time? Remember I saw you almost naked coming out of the shithouse with that ridiculous gun that does not work anymore. I can read you like a book." He stops and laughs, slapping his thighs with his big ringed hands. "When I close my eyes and picture you back at that lousy cabin looking for bears in your girly-girl see-through gown I am in stitches. You are a gutsy girl, I must admit and I love you for it." He wipes his eyes and turns all business like. "Now I want you to tell me the whole story. Who is this young chap to you, another one of your conquests, you old vamp?"

That darned Tony is playing me. I don't like it. I don't care how much I fear him, I am going to let him have it. He has succeeded in getting me mad as hell.

"Who are you, you snivelling scum bag! You left me a widow with all the debts to repay and you think that because you gave me a thousand bucks, you are off the hook? Don't underestimate me, I am old and decrepit but I can still teach you a lesson or two. If you want to know, Robin is my step son and I won't let you ruin him." I run to the kitchen to get the gun and point it right at him.

Just then the phone rings and I pick it up mechanically.

"Hello, MyDear" Cynthia bleats.

"Can't talk right now I am busy killing …cockroaches." Before I slam the phone back down I hear her say:"Oh Dear, coming right over." But I can't move, Tony has braced me from behind and he has grabbed the gun.

"Ha ha, you are caught because if I don't answer the door she will call the police!"

"Sit here like a good girl and don't you move, I will answer. If you don't behave I'll shoot her right in the eye." he says with an ominous look in his eyes. I sit.

He goes in the hall and I hear him say that he is my cousin; that I found a spider in the bathtub and I had a fit. Please come back in an hour. We have some family business to discuss.

He is right about the family business thing; it is family business. I am still so furious that I am not even scared of big fat Tony. If he shoots me, he will go down too because Cynthia is going to report him to the police. I will be dead but my unregistered will is in a safe and Robin will get a big chunk of my estate.

Tony sits down across from me nonchalantly waving the gun. He does not seem angry. It is too bad it will end like this because I found him rather fun to know, confident, smart and appealing in an odd sort of way. I hope Robin is not going to show up early.

"If you are going to kill me, do it fast, I am ready."

"We need to talk first. How did you get hold of this gun which happens to be mine?"

"That's none of your business."

"OK, fair enough. How did you meet Robin; have you known him long?"

"What is it to you?" I snarl.

He puts the gun on the coffee table within easy reach for me.

"I will do the talking then. Ed, your Edgar was an absolute blunderer; I apologize from the bottom of my heart for what happened to him. The stupid guy thought he was going to do business on the side. Your Ed was a poor excuse for a hoodlum. He was contacted by some extremely unpleasant characters bent on ruining the organization that I had built with care. It was and is as clean as an organization like this can be considering the political environment we now live in. I had notified him that he was out and as long as he kept his mouth shut he was safe. I found someone to replace him. My big mistake was to tell this new guy about Ed's defection. Believe me there are a lot of losers in this game. I did not trust Ed and his big mouth. So I sent this new fellow and his friend to scare him a little to make sure he would not blab. I did not and I repeat DID NOT have a contract out on him or on anyone else in all my life as you tend to believe. The next thing I knew is that you found him dead in his car. I am deeply sorry."

I am listening, eyeing the gun, ready to jump on it. Yet I must admit that as much as I loved him, Edgar was a dope and a desperate fool. He kept thinking that the odds would be in his favour. In some funky ways I am happy that the day he died he was sure that he had finally proved to himself that his theory was right. But he is dead and Robin is not.

Either Tony is a good actor or he is genuinely sorry. I can't tell.

"There are some things that I want you to understand; I conduct a very clean business, illegal maybe, but none the less very clean. My customers are not losers, they are respected members of the community. I have never sold tarnished products; I have never sold to children in the schools. My customers are lawyers, nurses, artists etc... People concerned about their health wanting to relax in a convivial atmosphere without the devastating after-effects of alcohol. For ulterior motives politicians and pharmaceutical companies have given cannabis a bad reputation, when doctors prescribe Ritalin to children as young as five years old, when you can buy over the counter so-called narcoleptics far more damaging to one's health than cannabis will ever be. I don't want to lecture you, I don't think I need to anyway. You are far too intelligent not to know. I offered Ed a good job and for a while he worked properly but he got in touch with some unsavoury characters, or rather they got in touch with him, and he was lured by the gains he thought he could make, the fuck-head. I fired him as soon as I heard about it. I was very sorry because he was a likeable guy."

"I want you to remember that I dearly loved this guy that you considered a fool. I loved him just for that because you are right, he was a dimwit. I loved his madness, his unpredictability. He was so different from most people I know. He didn't want money to get rich and respected; he wanted it to blow it away. He was capable of great generosity and would not have hurt a fly. Some people, like my father, are after status and recognition; Edgar just wanted to love and be loved."

"I envy you, Clara. You are so alive and you look pretty when you talk about Ed. Again I am sorry you got hurt so badly. This is why I do not want to hurt your Robin, who by the way is the spitting image of his father; I went out of my way to give him the job."

"So you knew that Robin is Edgar's son?"

"Of course, I made him talk when he came for the interview and I added it all up. I took a liking to him too, he is a fine fellow."

"Well, there is another guy you should fire, the one who just told Robin that you put a contract out on his father. I think you should talk to Robin, I hope for his sake that he will believe you like I do."

The gun is still on the coffee table. I get up and take it, Tony doesn't move.

"If you don't mind I will put this thing under lock and key, I can give you the key if you wish. You will get it back when things are cooler."

"I trust you. I will leave now, but make sure to call me to set up a meeting with Robin in a quiet public place if possible; perhaps it would be better if you are with him. Also I hope I can drop by your place once in a while, it is so refreshing talking with you. You make me feel good."

"You are welcome at any time, I lost my cooking touch but I make a mean cup of tea."

He hugs me and leaves.

I don't have time to think back on this very interesting conversation with Tony that Cynthia is at my door again.

"Well, my Dear, you never told me about your cousin, he is a handsome man and a good dresser."

"Sorry, Cynthia, I don't know why so many people seem to be showing up lately. Tony wanted to discuss a problem about our family tree. It made me upset recalling all those people who were not particularly nice characters. You know what families are like."

"Do I ever know, poor dear! I didn't want to interfere. I only wanted to ask you if you felt like going for lunch tomorrow."

"Not one of your fundraising affairs I hope?"

"No, no. I just remembered that we never had time to enjoy our dessert the last time we were out at that ill-chosen restaurant."

"That is a good idea. By the way, I need a favour from you. Could you be kind enough to retain this key for a while? It is the key for my safe. I keep my unregistered will in it until I find the time to make a new one properly. With all these visitors I would feel more comfortable if it is with you."

"No problems Clara, I am honoured by your trust."

I hand her the key of the safe where I just deposited the gun.

"Robin will be here soon. He is troubled by something and I want to have a long talk with him."

"Who is this young man to you, Clara? He acts as if he owns you." she inquires nosily.

"It is a long complicated story; I will tell you all about it soon Cynthia. Anyway I'll see you tomorrow at noon. You choose where, I'll do the driving. Any comfy joint will do except Casa di Antonio this time! Oh and no Chinese food, I don't want the fortune cookies either; I am done with predictions of any kind."

Cynthia leaves, not too soon for I am starting to feel exceedingly tired. All this action is not very good for my overall well-being. I phone Robin to tell him I have a touch of a cold and I am going to bed right now. He has the key to the apartment, so please not to wake me up. I'll see him bright and restored in the morning for breakfast. He sounds concerned and wonders if he should come back immediately. I beg him not to. I get my book and blissfully lie down on my bed with the bedroom door closed.

I must have slept around the clock. I can hear pots and pans being handled in the kitchen and Robin humming happily. I bet he is making the noise to wake me up, the big oaf. It's okay I feel rested, but I need to get my bearings before I face him. I don't have the chance because I see my bedroom door opening slowly, carefully, and through my half opened eyes I see the big curly head appear.

"OK, you can come in, I am kind of awake."

He leaps up and sits at the edge of the bed. "I made breakfast!" he toots.

"I guessed as much. You are a noisy cook."

"We are having pancakes with fresh blueberries and whipped cream, the bacon is in the oven, I was just wondering how many eggs you will eat," he announces proudly.

"Whoa, if we are going to live together, you will soon turn me into a blimp! After such a scrumptious breakfast I don't know how I am going to eat with Cynthia at noon. Maybe I should call her and cancel lunch."

"You better because I have lots to tell you."

"Oh no, not again, what is it this time, you are going to blow up a bank with your fancy gun?" I moan, teasing him because he is the true picture of happiness yet nonetheless I am a bit worried. I have heard these types of statements before from a fellow just like him. He takes my hand and pulls me out of bed. He is in his pyjamas, his curly hair all tousled and falling on his forehead; he looks like a big gangly kid and acts like one too. I don't think he is aware of his good looks. I am under his spell and this is why I allow myself to be dragged out of bed to the promised pancakes that I could have easily done without.

"Now here is your coffee and listen to me. I have so much to tell you!" he says with authority. He bangs a few more pots, a torture to my poor sleepy head and serves the pancakes with the trimmings. I am slumping on my chair, resigned to hear whatever. Yet after the first sip of the coffee he handed me, I straighten up; two sips of this brew he concocted and I will be ready to jump over buildings. I get up to mellow it down with hot water.

"Now, you have all my attention."

He sits burning with excitement. I live this as an umpteenth replay of what Edgar used to submit me to with the same devious look of satisfaction. Personality traits must be more deeply ingrained in the genes than we think. I must brace myself and keep an even keel to prevent Robin from shooting up into dreamland stars.

"First after you left me on campus, I decided to look for a former teacher that I liked; I was lucky, he was in his office. He recognized me and we started to chat. I asked him what he thought it would take for me to resume my studies after I explained what happened to me. He was kind enough to make a few phone calls to the registrar and such. It turns out that if this summer I would take two of the courses I flunked I could then, with hard work, finish my degree in one year. I was so happy about that! Can you imagine, Auntie, in one year I could enrol in a master's program? What do you think? Isn't that great?"

"I am absolutely delighted that you take returning to school so seriously, but above all with such amazing enthusiasm!" Yet there is a but to every good story and I know by experience that I have not heard it all.

"After I left the teacher's office, I was so happy, I decided to go look in the library to check if I could not find any old friends. Bill was there just getting out when I arrived. We got to talking and he invited me for a drink at his place that he shares with his sister."

"I knew it, I knew it. There had to be a girl in the story!" I exclaim with a wink.

"Oh, Auntie, she looks just like you!"

"I hope not, poor girl, old before her time!"

"She has green eyes and red hair; she is kind of short with a great body. She is doing her masters degree as a librarian. She is shy but has a great smile. I invited her for a coffee tomorrow. You know what? She said she would love that. Isn't that nice?"

"It is positively astounding!" I reply tongue in cheek. It doesn't matter what I say, he is on cloud nine but I have to pull him down for we have to settle the Tony business as soon as possible. He is pacing back and forth in the kitchen, banging a few more pots on the way. I finish my cup of coffee and announce that I will be in the bathroom getting ready.

"But you have not finished your breakfast!"

"You finish it for me dear Robin."

He sits down and starts gulping down the mountain of pancakes as if it was to be his very last meal; I diplomatically exit the kitchen. He must have been starving for affection, the poor boy. I have been so busy myself with my drastic life change that I have not given him the support I now realize he desperately needed. I have been too cocooned too long in my little world of selfishness.

While deliciously soaking in my bath water I am pondering on the deep down reason of my callousness. Maybe after Edgar's death I closed up to grieve but also because I didn't think I could be or I wanted to be of any use to anyone. It could also be that I am victim of my own ageist biases. Anyway, enough pondering and philosophising, I must bring Robin to Tony. This is of paramount urgency for the young man's sake.

He is knocking on the bathroom door.

"Auntie, I forgot to tell you that I invited Sarah here this afternoon. I really want you two to meet."

"It is OK, Robin, but I must make a few phone calls first. I will be out in a short spell. We need to get organized." I yell back. I better cancel that lunch with Cynthia.

Once in my bedroom, out of earshot of Robin, I first call Cynthia and then Tony. Cynthia is not impressed, she was looking forward to our little lark. Tony says that after thinking about our conversation the best place to meet with Robin would be in his office downtown either today or tomorrow afternoon. The earlier the better.

It takes some heavy duty artillery to get Robin to finally agree to go and see Tony. He is definitely not interested in any reprisals against Tony, all his thoughts are on seducing the girl of his heart returning to his studies and making a life for himself as he calls it. Bury the hatchet.

At eleven Robin and I reach Tony's office. On the door there is a golden sign announcing him as an investing counsellor. Nice friendly receptionist telling us that her boss will be with us in a short while. True enough, five minutes later she ushers us into Tony's office.

"So, my boy, how are you doing? So glad to see you! First let me tell you that you are doing a fine job up there. Congratulations!" he shakes his hand vigorously in a most convivial way.

Robin is jittery, his eyes downcast, as if he is searching for an answer on the carpet, a far cry from the happy-go-lucky young man at breakfast. Tony invites us to sit on very comfortable armchairs and crosses over to his desk; I notice that the top drawer is slightly ajar. Clever Tony. I am sure he has a gun in there. Never too cautious. I can see why Tony is a survivor in this cutthroat business.

"So, what can I do for you?" he asks in what seems like genuine concern. "I have another appointment in half an hour but these thirty minutes are yours. So let's get down to business. You wanted to see me..." he adds.

There is no doubt in my mind that Tony is taking the lead in this conversation and he is bent on solving the problem no matter what. I better put my two cents in before the two heads high on testosterone begin ramming against each other, and I know who will win. Robin doesn't stand a chance.

"To start off, Tony, I did not tell Robin about our former conversation. We just discussed the possibility of him returning to university to finish his degree, since I am now, as you know in a position to finance him for the two years of studies he still needs to do. He claims he can't do it because he owes you money and he is committed to the job you offered him. I am wondering what it would take to release him of his commitment." I give myself a virtual pat on the back for being so smooth.

Robin is ensconced in the armchair and incommunicado. Tony closes his eyes elbows on his desk and holds his hands together tapping his fingers. Dead silence. I wait, eyeing the top desk drawer. Then Tony opens half of his left eye, "Robin, where is that gun I lent you?"

"It's at Auntie Clara's" Robin says with a guilty look on his face.

"It's in my safe and my friend Cynthia has the only key." I add looking at Tony straight in the face.

I am relieved to see Tony closing the top desk drawer. I never get it out of my mind that this guy is ruthless in spite of his late middle-aged debonair look. Again he would not be where he is now if it were otherwise.

"Robin, you have proven to me that you are a good reliable worker; I am very pleased with your work. I am happy that I trusted you even though you look so much like your father."

Robin perks up. "You have no idea what you are talking about!" he hissed aggressively.

"Oh, yes I do. Physically you are his spitting image. Let's call a spade a spade and cut out the bullshit. I liked Ed. I am sorry he died the way he did. He was a fun guy but the worst businessman I have ever known, forever trying to beat the odds. While he was doing the same job for me that I entrusted you with, he owed a lot of gambling money to some goons who were my competitors at the time. He came to beg me to bail him out. For me it was once too many times. I refused and fired him to teach him a lesson. I also told him to get some help for his problem. I thought by doing so he would clean up his act and come back to me with a better attitude. Little did I know that he had promised delivery of my goods to them and at the last minute did not comply. I sent a kid, a new recruit, to monitor him. That is how I know how he died. I did not put a contract out on him nor did I want him dead. In spite of all his failings he was a good egg, with a heart of gold. When you showed up asking me for a job, I was delighted to help out to belatedly honour his memory. Now tell me what else I can do for you."

Tony has been talking in a monotonous tone pausing, searching for words. Against my will, what he says rings true. Yet it does not matter whether it is true or not; Edgar is dead but Robin is not and I must protect him. I sense him cogitating beside me; I hope that he can see that it is to his advantage to believe what he has just been told. I think I should throw in some incentives.

"What I am wondering, Tony, is if and how you could relieve Robin of the agreement he has with you? I would very much like him to finish his degree and he can't do it from Prince Rupert."

"Dear Clara, I want to hear it from him. He is a grown man and my employee and I expect him to behave as such. He must strike a deal with me, not through a third party. I want a man-to-man talk. As a matter of fact I would prefer you leave my office. I have had enough of this attitude!" All that said in a gentlemanly fashion. I leave Robin in the lion's den and go wait for him downstairs, past the receptionist with her frozen smile and across the street to a coffee shop where I can sit comfortably near the window to be able to notice Robin when he steps out of Tony's office building. I sense Robin is in need of a good fatherly shake that I am incapable of giving to him. I trust Tony will do just that.

While sipping my cup of coffee, I reflect on what happened. I have got to admit Tony is right, Robin has an attitude. He was behaving like a teenager, much younger than his actual age. Sometimes I am not even sure who, of Jeo or Robin, is the oldest. I wonder if this is the outcome of a fatherless upbringing or if it is Edgar's genes. Yet I find this young man very compelling in his childlike behavior. He has what I would call a clean soul. I do hope that Tony the fox sees that too and will be inclined as I am to protect him.

And now, here he is stepping out of the building. I observe his gait carefully for signs of dismay or elation. I step out of the coffee shop to hail him. He rushes to me, embraces me in one of his crushing bear hugs. I am breathless and happy to be. A welcomed new life is starting for both of us. There is some planning to do but that can wait until tomorrow. For now let's enjoy the rain, the gray sky and the freedom from squalid worries. I am creating my family of choice. Aristotle was right after all with his theory of spontaneous generation, my new life was born of a chance encounter with a Persian cat, no egg involved.

Robin is practically dancing alongside me. The deal is that he has to work for Tony until the end of August and properly train his replacement. He will only get half of his income the other half will go toward his debts. If he wants to take the two courses he flunked he will have to make arrangements with the university and take them by correspondence.

"He must have a lot of respect for you because he told me that if ever the occasion arises where he would have to choose between you and me, he would side with you without a doubt." Robin confides.

Epilogue

Seven months have passed. It is now August. Beautiful, flowery summer. I have been going back and forth to Prince Rupert to encourage Robin and visit my beloved Jeo and his family. The little girl, Morgan, is starting school in September and so is her mother June. Merle and Winston the cat appear and disappear on my horizon as they see fit. We have a lovely relationship, no strings attached.

Cynthia, dear Cynthia, is slacking a bit in her involvement with the Who-is-Who. She does not like the trend politics takes these days. I try to nudge her to resume her activism with greater fervour by praising the virtues of chicken a la king and long winded self-congratulating eulogies mostly to keep her out of my hair. I even went with her once or twice to help her renew her 'outdated' wardrobe. I wear a lot of her hand-me-downs. She has a thing against Merle but never tarries on the good looks and gentlemanly qualities of my 'cousin' Tony who, true to his words, shows up now and then for a cup of tea; blueberry tarts are generously supplied by my enthusiastic neighbour.

I also got rid of a lot of Macky's gadgets. Some of the wall-hangings I gave to a gay bridge club on the condition that they also hang a plaque to acknowledge his memory. They were most thankful. I have made sure that my will is duly registered. I named Tony as my executor.

Robin is moving in in a few days now. He is head over heels in love with Sarah, who I must admit is a very nice girl. She has a head on her shoulders which is a blessing for Robin. Tony is adamant that I should not let her move in with Robin at my place. Although he is all for the relationship, he believes that if they want to live together they should act like adults and not like parasitic nincompoops. I fully agree. It is strange but also delightful to see Tony in an almost father-son relationship with Robin. This Tony has a heart even so he hides it well under a coat of aloofness. Of all the people I have met in the past year, Tony is the one I trust the most.

I have been doing all this recap of my last year since I met the cat, while getting ready for the first big solo jump with my own rainbow coloured brand new paraglider. I have been taking lessons on the sly, not telling anybody because I did not want to alarm anyone or be dissuaded by any of these people who now crowd my life. I had to lie a bit about my age to the instructors. I am pleased to have found the cream of the crop in terms of instructions.

I am alone at the top of the mountain, one hundred meters from the cliff drop. My equipment is ready, but I must wait until I regain my breath after climbing the last part of the mountain lugging my gear on my back. The last tandem flight I did lasted over two hours. I want to do the same alone without telling a soul.

I have my variometer to help me detect air currents, climb- or sink-rates and altitude. I also have my cell phone, no GPS though. All these toys are courtesy of Macky's legacy. I thank him from the bottom of my heart; I also have in one of my numerous pockets a little bit of his ashes that I intend to spread over what I will consider the most beautiful spot. I feel that I, and all the others that will benefit from his last will, owe him this symbolic gesture.

The wind is ideal. I have dealt with my Thens and the possible Afters. It is time for me to be in the surprising Now. I choose to do a reverse launch. It is easier to inspect the wing and check that the lines are free as it leaves the ground; also if I slip during launching I will fall forward rather than backward. But mostly it requires far less effort from my old legs.

Two tries and I am off the ground. I am flying. What a wonderful experience! Three hundred meters above sea level according to my variometer. Down below the mighty river flows toward the sea. An eagle circles above to inspect me and my iridescent wing.

An electrifying feeling of joy pervades every cell in my body. I am floating, a tiny entity at one with the universe, so dependant and yet so free. I sense the intimate tie with everyone of my newly found family:

Cynthia the aggravating sister; my brother the poor luckless clown Macky; Robin my chivalrous wit deficient son, Jeo the impish little dreamer; powerful Morgan the conjuror; June the swooning princess; Harvey the silent guardian of his paradise; crafty Tony my cousin; Merle my medicine man; and Winston the princely fat cat my consort - thinking about it that furry sneak reminds me a lot of Tony; I love them all, even Marge with her crooked mouth and loose dentures. I am proud to be an integral part of the ever irredeemable silly human race and deeply thankful to Mother Earth for keeping me enthralled by her lasting beauty and generosity. Amen!

I let go of Macky's ashes over the tree tops. I try all the stunts my instructors taught me. It works. That old head of mine is not totally decrepit after all. Following the air currents I rise and turn and plunge to rise again. I am laughing, this is total bliss. Now exhausted with an overdose of glee, it is the time for the spiral dive - a descent of ten meters per second...

Disorientation...

Blackout...

The cat did it.